LEARNING CURVES

A First Edition Omnibus

CEILLIE SIMKISS

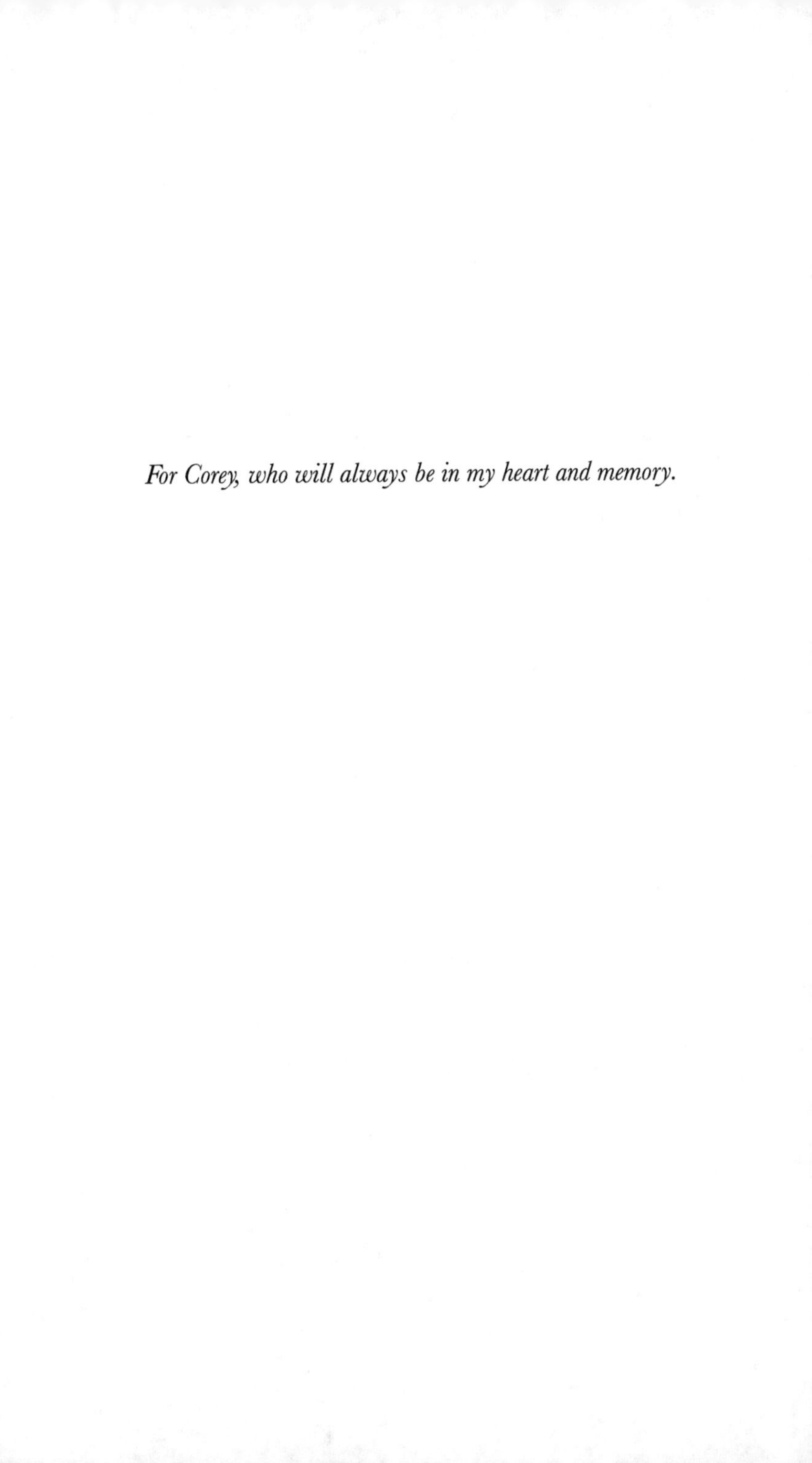

For Corey, who will always be in my heart and memory.

Consolidated Content Notes

THIS IS INTENDED to help people be as comfortable as they can when reading these stories, and if that's not necessary for you, that's fine! If you believe that content notes are spoilers, I advise that you ignore this section.

Learning Curves:

Learning Curves contains: mentions of homophobia, mentions of aphobia, worries about and mentions of ableism, discussion of food and cooking, family members showing up unannounced, and an on page panic attack.

Wrapped Up In You

Wrapped Up In You contains a lot of food and the eating of it, and Christmas celebrations.

The Ghosts of Halloween

The Ghosts of Halloween contains: an on page panic attack from the POV character in Present, discussion of pregnancy between two cisgender women in Future

The Final Interview

It contains pre-job interview anxiety from the POV character.

IF THERE ARE other content notes that you believe should be applied to any of the stories in this omnibus please send me an email at admin@foxglovefiction.com and it can be added to this list.

LEARNING CURVES

CEILLIE SIMKISS

Cover Artist: Les Solot

Elena Mendez has always been career-first; with only two semesters of law school to go, her dream of working as a family lawyer for children is finally within reach. She can't afford distractions. She doesn't have time for love.

And she has no idea how much her life will change, the day she lends her notes to Cora McLaughlin.

A freelance writer and MBA student, Cora is just as career-driven as Elena. But over weeks in the library together, they discover that as strong as they are apart, they're stronger together. Through snowstorms and stolen moments, through loneliness and companionship, the two learn they can weather anything as long as they have each other—even a surprise visit from Elena's family.

From solitude to sweetness, there's nothing like falling in love. College may be strict…but when it comes to love, Cora and Elena are ahead of the learning curve.

~

$$\rule{3in}{0.4pt}$$

Chapter 1

$$\rule{3in}{0.4pt}$$

FLUORESCENT LIGHTS BOUNCED off of the whitewashed cinder block walls in the hallway of the Bryan Building. It seemed excessively bright compared to the matte gray that stretched across Greensboro's skyline as it did on most October mornings, and Elena found herself squinting a little.

Her head was full of thoughts of the business law class she'd just left, and she was operating mostly on autopilot when an unfamiliar voice said her name.

"Hey, Elena, right?"

Elena turned, taking care not to knock her large bag into the other people in the hallway. She found a short, slim woman at her elbow looking at her nervously. The other woman was familiar, but Elena wasn't quite sure where she knew her from.

As she stared at the woman wearing a long-sleeved flannel shirt-dress while other graduate students flowed around them in the hallway, something clicked in Elena's head — this was one of the girls from her business law class.

"Yeah. You're Cora, right?" Elena mentally crossed her fingers, hoping that was her name. Seeing her nod, Elena continued. "What's up?"

"I've noticed you always do really well on the quizzes and stuff. How good are your notes?" She ran a hand through her blonde hair, nearly shaved on the sides, but with a small pompadour of tight curls on the top, pink tingeing her freckled cheeks. She was the kind of girl who Elena would have guessed to be queer on first glance, between the flannel and undercut.

"Pretty good, why?"

"I, um, kind of hyperfocused on James singing to himself in the back of class today and couldn't keep up with class at the same time. Is there any way you could email me your notes? Or I could copy them from you, or-"

Elena cut her off with a short wave. Cora's entire face was bright red now. There was no reason to make her suffer any more embarrassment, especially in a crowded college hallway full of their classmates.

"I take all my notes on my laptop. I can email them to you. What's your email address?"

Cora's face lit up, showing off her slightly crooked teeth. Elena couldn't keep a matching one from spreading across her own face. Cora handed over a folded sheet of notebook paper with her email address written on it in clear block letters, which Elena folded and tucked into the large purse she carried.

"I'll send them to you when I get to lunch in a few minutes. James is a terrible singer, and I don't think he knows." Elena rolled her eyes in commiseration. James was one of her fellow law students, and she had purposely sat as far away from him as possible in the thirty person classroom. "All of our other professors have banned him from singing in class, but I guess Doctor Burgess hasn't noticed yet or just doesn't care."

"Ugh," she moaned. "It's the worst. I wish I hadn't sat next to him, even if that seat did have the best light. Priorities, right?"

Cora widened her eyes and grimaced in an expression that Elena found strangely adorable.

"I'm ADHD and even with meds, stuff like that can really screw me on a bad day," Cora continued. She rubbed her fingers through the short-cropped hair in front of her ear. Her expression turned rueful.

"That's probably more than you needed to know about the girl begging for your notes. I'll let you get to lunch. I know they keep you law kids on a really tight schedule. Thank you again for the notes, Elena. I really appreciate it."

"It's not a problem. We all have bad days," Elena said reassuringly. "You should have an email from me within the hour."

"Thank you thank you thank you!" She began to walk away, then turned and waved goodbye. Elena's heart skipped a beat.

Walking across the campus to the dining hall, Elena found herself wondering why she hadn't ever talked to the girl before. She was the kind of girl whose aesthetic Elena loved, and she seemed really nice. Then she remembered — she didn't really talk to anybody in the class, except when required. Cora hadn't been wrong about the law students being incredibly busy, and most of Elena's classmates were problematic at best.

Business law was one of the hardest classes to get into at the university they attended. It was a required class for both business and law graduate students at the University of North Carolina at Greensboro. There were never enough sections of it offered for the number of students who had to take it. There were barely enough seats in the classroom for everyone who needed to be in it.

However, it was also one of the only classes that didn't have group projects, which was a relief. Group projects were only helpful if you were a slacker because you could figure out who usually did the work. Elena was usually that person and thus hated group work.

Elena slotted herself into one of the cafeteria chairs that had been designed for much slimmer people than she was. Chairs with molded arms always were. Settling in, she pulled out her laptop and closed the extraneous programs to get to her email.

With a flash of brilliance as she checked her notes for spelling errors, she remembered that there was a free seat on the far side of her self-assigned desk in the classroom. Elena smoothed down the Puerto Rican flag sticker that covered the area next to her laptop's trackpad. Smiling, she typed out an email, attaching the notes.

To: Cora (cemclaughlin@uncg.edu);

From: Elena (emmendez@uncg.edu);

Subject: Bus Law Notes

Hey, Cora,

This is Elena from Business Law with the notes you asked for. Hope these are helpful for you. Let me know if there's any shorthand in here that doesn't make sense, and I'll try and translate it to you.

I remembered as I sat down that there's a free seat next to me by the door, from when that greasy kid dropped out of the program. James is always noisy, so if you wanted to start sitting there, I wouldn't mind. I'd love to get to know you better.

Sincerely,

Elena

Gnawing her lower lip, Elena stared at the email for a few moments, wondering if the last sentence was too forward. Shaking her head at herself, she hit send. Cora would want to be friends or not - Elena being too forward in an email wouldn't change anything but how long it took them to figure it out. She wondered if being forward was even a thing people worried about anymore.

Elena took a deep breath in through her nose and remembered how hungry she was. Dining hall food was no comparison to the homemade food she'd grown up making and eating, but it would do for a working lunch. Elena slid her laptop back into her bag and made her way towards the food, her heart thumping slightly at the idea of making a new friend.

BY THE TIME the next class rolled around, Elena had almost forgotten that she'd told Cora about the empty seat. The much shorter girl had already set up her laptop in the seat directly between Elena's usual seat and the wall. And... there was a clear plastic cup of iced coffee sitting on Elena's desk?

"Is someone sitting there?" Elena asked quietly, blinking several times in rapid succession.

"Oh, hey!" Cora jumped a little in her seat, her cheeks coloring a little in clear embarrassment.

"No, no one's sitting there. Um, that's for you? I used to work as a barista and noticed that you bring mocha frappucinos to class a lot, so I wanted to thank you."

"Oh!" Elena made a sound of surprise and set her bag on the ground. "I didn't realize you'd been watching me so carefully. I didn't have a chance to get coffee this morning, so this is perfect! Thanks so much!"

"You're welcome. Your color-coded notes were the only reason I know most of the stuff that's gonna be on the test this week." Cora's cheeks turned an even deeper pink, making her freckles stand out. "I'm hoping that sitting over here will be a game changer for me. I've been struggling with James' singing under his breath all semester and I didn't realize this seat had opened up."

"I think the kid who sat here dropped out entirely last week? I don't even know his name. Either way, I promise there won't be any singing," Elena laughed lightly. "Dr. Burgess also teaches a couple of my other classes, and my notes are probably the only reasons I've passed them all so far. She's a hardass, but she's a great teacher."

"She seems like it. I'm in the MBA program, so the law aspect is less critical for me to know offhand, but it's really interesting, as weird as that sounds."

"That doesn't sound weird at all!" Elena smiled back, glad to know that someone other than her found joy in different aspects of the law. "The law is really intricate and specific, which is why I love it."

She looked like she wanted to say more, but Dr. Burgess swept in and slammed the door of the classroom. The professor threw her purse on the desk at the front of the classroom, and Elena and Cora exchanged wide-eyed glances.

The entire class sat up just a little bit straighter, and aside from the noises of breathing and shuffling, was absolutely silent.

"Hello, class." Dr. Burgess huffed. "Take out a pen and some paper. Pop quiz time."

The class groaned in unison before moving to take

out something to write with and on. Elena wondered what had bit her to get her in such a mood today.

Cora had been typing furiously on her laptop, and Elena felt her phone buzz in her blazer pocket. While pulling out her notebook and setting herself up for the quiz, Elena checked her phone and saw an email.

To: Elena

From: Cora

I like your flag sticker. Want to get lunch later? Here's my number. (336) 555-5555

Elena glanced sideways at Cora. She guessed she hadn't been too forward last week. Catching Cora's eye, she nodded, and the other girl's entire face lit up. Elena's heart skipped a beat again, and she couldn't help but smile back.

ELENA HAD JUST CLOSED the door behind herself in her apartment when she felt her phone vibrate in the pocket of her maxi skirt. She pulled it out to find a picture of her mother on the screen.

It was a photo that radiated joy - a huge smile on Maria's wide brown face, with her head thrown back and the summer sun glinting off of her forehead. It was one of Elena's favorites.

She tossed her keys into a bowl on the short dark wood bookshelf by the door, set her backpack down next to it, and swiped to answer the phone call

"Hola Mamá," she sang into the phone. "How are you today?"

"Well, somebody is cheerful," Maria laughed. "Cómo estás, mija?"

"I'm good, Mamá! Something crawled up Doctor

Burgess's butt today, and we had a really difficult pop quiz, but otherwise, it's a pretty good day. I actually had lunch with a classmate."

"A classmate, eh?" She could hear her mother's thick eyebrows rising to her hairline despite the distance between them. "Is it a girl?"

Elena felt a blush rise to her cheeks. "Maaaaaybe?"

"Oh, a girl! How delightful. What is her name? Tell me all about her!"

She could hear Maria settling into her favorite armchair, and could picture her resting her chin in one hand, her elbow on the arm of the chair, and the phone in her other hand. She was in full on gossip mode, and Elena couldn't help but laugh.

"I've only talked to her twice! I don't know that much about her yet."

"Well, you haven't even told me her name yet, mija! Surely you know that much?"

Elena rolled her eyes.

"Her name is Cora, Mamá. Give me a second to strip and then I'll spill all the details."

As soon as the words left her mouth she realized her mistake. Before she could correct herself, her mother's voice went stricken.

"Elena Maria! Where are you that you are stripping? Do you need more money? It is too cold for that!"

"No, Mamá, I didn't actually mean stripping! I just meant taking off my coat and things! I just got home and it's warm in here."

"Oh. Well, anyway, tell me about this girl as soon as you have stripped."

Maria could apparently sense the eye roll that was impending.

"Do not roll your eyes at me, young lady! I may not be present but I am still your mother!"

Now Elena had to roll her eyes as she kicked off the wedge heels she'd worn to class. They made a satisfying thunk against the wall and Elena sighed.

"While I'm getting undressed, why don't you tell me about your day? What's going on with you?"

"Ah, a little bit of this, a little bit of that. I went grocery shopping today, and the eggs were so expensive! Almost $2 for a dozen! Es ridículo, no?"

She shook her head. That was significantly more expensive than usual for October.

"That really is ridiculous. Where were you shopping? Did you go to Whole Foods again?"

"No! Well, yes, I did go to Whole Foods. They have the lactose-free ice cream your Papi likes. But I was looking at eggs at Aldi on…. Randleman Road, I think? The usual one on the less expensive side of town."

"I see," Elena said, pulling her sweater over her head. The collar caught on her helix piercing and she winced. Her mother continued.

"And of course I had to buy them! I cannot cook without eggs, now can I? Your Papi needs his breakfast whether it is expensive or not. But why are they expensive? Did all the chickens stop laying or something?"

"I don't know, Mamá. But I'm glad you got the eggs for Papi. I'm sure he will appreciate them."

"Bah, it is my job. If I sent him to the store, we would come home with all organic foods every time, half of them made of granola. And two of everything!"

Elena laughed. She knew it was true. If she sent her father to the store for one very specific item, he would come back with two or three "for later" or the organic version, if it existed.

"Have you finished undressing yet, mija? I want to hear about this girl."

She was close. She wanted to get into her pajamas, but she supposed that could wait.

"Don't emphasize girl like that, Mamá. She's cute and sweet, but it's not like that."

"Not like that ye-et," Maria sang into the phone, stretching 'yet' into two syllables. "So her name is Cora, and she's sweet and cute. What is her degree in?"

Elena poured herself a glass of water and wandered over to her loveseat, tucking one of her legs and settled in.

"So, she's getting her MBA and she does a lot of freelance writing. I'm honestly not sure how she manages everything she says she does on top of school. She's ADHD and very pretty."

"I see! What kind of pretty is she? I assume since her name is Cora she's white?"

"Yeah, she's kind of a stereotypical white queer girl - she's slim and blue-eyed with curly hair. She keeps it pretty close shaved on the sides, so she doesn't fidget with it."

"She sounds pretty. Does she have a cat? She sounds like the kind of girl I would expect to have a cat. Or three. You know you are very allergic to cats."

Her mother wasn't wrong. She'd been known to break out in hives from even being in a room that had held a cat in the last few days. Luckily, that wasn't a problem here.

"She doesn't have a cat. She wants a dog, but wants to wait until she graduates in the spring and will have more time for it."

She could hear Maria nodding through the phone.

"She seems sensible. I like this Cora."

Elena couldn't keep a smile from spreading across her face at her mother's approval.

"I'm glad to hear that, Mamá. I really am."

Chapter 2

OVER THE NEXT FEW WEEKS, Cora and Elena fell into an easy routine. They'd walk to the dining hall together after class for lunch, and talk about anything and everything from the antics of their classmates to the books Cora had been reading.

They took turns sending ridiculous selfies to their siblings and parents, reassuring all that they had only fallen into the depths of grad school, not off the face of the earth.

Elena caught herself giggling at her phone when Cora texted her throughout the day. Cora had taken to joining Elena in the library for long studying sessions, usually bringing some sort of fast food for them both, her laptop and at least three books for work or for pleasure.

Whatever Cora brought with her, Elena was glad for the company. The food was usually less satisfying than Elena wanted it to be, but given that they were college students and it had to be able to be eaten either warm or cold, they worked with what they could get.

"Why do you always bring your own books with

you?" Elena asked one day when they were working together in the library and Cora pulled a book out of her purse. "We're literally in a place that has books. For free. Why do you need more?"

Cora's eyebrows knit together, and she pulled the book to her chest protectively.

"The library doesn't have the right books," she said with a pout. "This library only has academic stuff. I want fun - magic, dragons, queer people. The works!"

"Okay that's fair," Elena admitted. "But why do you read them at the library?"

"I don't really have anywhere else I need to be," Cora said with a shrug. "Plus, I like hanging out with you, even if we are just doing classwork."

Elena tilted her head curiously. Surely there was someone else Cora wanted to hang out with.

"Don't you have other people, though?" Elena asked. "There's no way I'm your only friend. You're too neat not to have anybody here!"

Cora's mouth twisted, and her eyes dropped back to the orange book that was sitting on the table between them. She didn't answer for a moment, instead drawing small circles on the book cover with her finger.

"Not so much. I moved here for school, and I had a boyfriend and a few friends in the city. The boyfriend didn't work out and I kind of lost contact with most of them. My roommates are neat, but they're pre-med and engineering, and also have boyfriends. They're pretty busy."

"Oh." Elena almost regretted asking the question, even if she did want to know the answer. Cora clearly didn't want to talk about it.

"Well, I'm glad you're here - even if you're the only

person I've ever met that brings books to the library that don't belong here."

"They're books, you heathen!" Cora gave an exaggeratedly pretentious sniff while simultaneously shooting Elena a teasing glare. "They belong everywhere, much like myself!"

Elena smiled widely. There was the cheery woman she knew and adored. She blinked a little, realizing that she did adore Cora.

"Hell yeah, you do. I'm glad you choose to hang out with my queer ass on a regular basis. You're pretty great." Elena smiled shyly, and Cora returned it with a smile so wide that it made her nose wrinkle.

"Yeah, yeah. Don't you have homework you should be doing?" Cora's tone was chiding, but the smile took all the sting out of it.

As Elena watched, Cora glanced back down at the book she was still clutching to her chest, and one of her curls had flopped forward into her face. She set the book lightly on the table and shook the curl back into place as she raised her head, still smiling. Elena was still watching her.

"I'd think that was more important than staring at my silly face."

Elena's face turned bright pink.

"I'm totally working."

Her normally deep voice had raised an entire octave, and she had started digging through the pile of textbooks with a vigor she hadn't had a few moments ago.

"I don't know what you're talking about!"

Cora's smile turned into a smirk, and Elena knew she was letting her have the lie.

∼

A FEW WEEKS LATER, Elena stared sadly at the dining hall cheese fries that Cora had brought to munch on while they worked. Finally, Elena threw her pen down. It bounced off the book she was working from and into the sad tub of fries. The cheese was so plasticized that you could use it as a mirror.

Cora giggled.

"Are you doing anything tonight?" Elena asked.

Cora set her book down face down, careful not to wrinkle the pages and looked at Elena quizzically.

"I'd planned on being here until we quit studying, so I guess not?"

"I haven't cooked in weeks," Elena sighed dramatically. She usually cooked at least a few dishes on the weekends. "No offense, Cora, but I'm tired of eating boring white people food. I want proper food. I want sancocho and water bread!"

"I have no idea what sancocho is, but I'll try anything if you know where to get it?" Cora replied, sounding hesitant but brave. "Is it Puerto Rican? Is there a good restaurant to get it in Greensboro?"

"It's like beef stew, but better, but there isn't a good Puerto Rican restaurant here," Elena chewed on the inside of her lip while she thought. "Luckily, Mamá taught all four of us how to cook like a proper Puerto Rican housewife. I need to cook something and get away from these textbooks or I'm going to explode."

"Well, we can't have you exploding!" Cora giggled, a sound Elena adored. "I'm guessing since you haven't cooked in a while, you'll need to go grocery shopping. Want to go now?"

Elena's eyes lit up with excitement.

"Yes! Let's go!"

They packed up their bags quickly, clearing the room

in record time, and walked toward the exterior doors of the library as quickly as they could without actually running.

Passing the double doors, they both burst into giggles, leaning toward each other with the effort of trying to catch their breath.

"Why are we moving so fast?" Elena asked breathily.

"I have no idea!" Cora laughed. "But it seemed like the right thing to do!"

AFTER A QUICK BUT productive trip to the grocery store, Elena had gathered all of the ingredients for sancocho and splurged on a bottle of an oaky Italian red wine that she knew would pair well with the beef in the stew.

The two women had driven to Elena's small apartment and lined up the group of ingredients so that everything was where Elena wanted it to be. She surveyed it with a practiced eye, rearranging the bags of vegetables and beef until she was satisfied.

"This is a lot of vegetables for one pot of stew," Cora noted with a hint of skepticism. "Do you always put corn on the cob in yours?"

Elena tsked and glanced at her sideways. "That's one of the most important ingredients, girl! Corn on the cob is what makes it Puerto Rican! The corn soaks up all of the flavors from the beef and the sazón. Mm!"

"I'm not usually a veggie person..." Cora was sitting on a barstool in front of the counter, looking skeptically at the bags of vegetables sitting in front of her.

"You won't even know you're eating veggies once the

sazón gets in there." Elena asserted, pulling her hair into a high ponytail. "I bet you 20 bucks you'll like it."

"I'll take that bet," Cora cocked an eyebrow at the larger woman. "In the meantime, gimme a knife and tell me what to do!"

"Sweet," Elena smiled widely, her tongue resting between the rows of her teeth.

She pulled a knife out of the block on the counter, and slid a cutting board over to the short girl where she sat.

"You can chop the onion and green pepper while I cut up this beef. One small onion should do it, just nicely chopped. It doesn't need to be that small. No crying, though. The kitchen is for cleansing the soul."

"Pfft." Cora began to chop the onion. "I don't cry. I'm a grown woman."

"Okay, first of all, you can't say you don't cry. You just cried yesterday in the library because a character in your book died." Elena pointed out, to Cora's embarrassment. "Second of all, you have to cry sometimes. It's good for you"

"My book was sad, okay? He was a rogue with a heart of gold, and they killed him. You know they're my favorite!" Cora stuck her tongue out, and immediately regretted her decision. "Well, that was a mistake. Now my whole mouth tastes like onion, blah!"

Her face wrinkled in disgust and Elena burst into laughter. Cora's tongue was darting between her lips trying to get rid of the onion flavor that had snuck in.

"You're a hot mess, Cora," Elena declared through her giggles.

"At least I'm hot, then. You invited me to dinner, so it's good enough for me!"

Elena shook her head at her friend's silly remark and

pulled out a mixing bowl. She set it on the counter for Cora to put the onions in when she was done dicing, and turned back to the stove.

The two women fell into a companionable silence, chopping vegetables and watching the pan. Hisses and sizzles soon filled the air alongside the smell of searing beef, onions, and garlic.

"Is your apartment always this quiet?" Cora asked as she finished chopping her last pepper before she folded the plastic cutting board and tilted it into the bowl with the rest of the veggies. Tossing fresh cilantro on top of it all, she passed the bowl to Elena.

"I'm not much for loud music," Elena said as she added the vegetables to the cast iron Dutch oven that would soon hold the sancocho. "It makes me really anxious, and being in relative quiet really helps me calm down."

"I can understand that," Cora said with an easy shrug "Are your neighbors always this quiet, too? That's unusual in student housing, even an end unit apartment."

Elena had expected a different question, and filled the pause by wiping her sweaty forehead on her upper arm.

"Yeah, they're very nice. I really got lucky with this apartment. Can you get the beef stock out of the fridge?" Elena asked. The shorter girl did as she was asked. She twisted the lid off the top, and handed the box of stock to her. "This would be better if I'd had time to make my own stock, but that is not meant to be today."

"I'm sure it'll still be delicious, El."

Out of the corner of her eye, Elena caught Cora smiling at her while she poured the stock into the pot.

Setting the bottle down, she moved back to her cutting board and knife.

"How much of this butternut squash do I need to cut up?"

"Half of it, in like one-inch cubes. And the plátanos need to be sliced in one-inch slices as well. I've got the potatoes to peel and cube, the corn to slice and the yucca to dice. Sound good?"

"Sounds good!"

Both women went back to chopping while they waited for the stock to reduce, all of the sliced and diced vegetables going into the bowl that stood between them on the counter.

"What made you want to be a lawyer?" Cora asked out of nowhere, keeping her eyes focused on the plantain in her hand. Elena looked up at her, her eyes serious.

"Mamá was a foster parent for a long time. Most of the kids that came to us were the ones who were 14 or 15, and maybe had a little bit of an attitude. We'd have the social workers telling us that they couldn't get emancipated from their parents, so they were stuck in foster care. Nobody wanted to adopt them because new parents want to adopt cute kids, not teenagers."

Elena could tell that her face was getting red with an anger she'd had for as long as she could remember, and she could feel her chest heaving. She took a few deep breaths, trying to calm herself down. Cora looked at her, concern etched in the wrinkles on her forehead.

"Sorry, I don't usually get this upset in front of people."

Cora made to pat her on the shoulder or hold her hand, but Elena waved her away.

"Anyway, we helped Everett, one of the kids that lived with us, get emancipation after he turned 16 with the help of a family lawyer," She explained. "That kicked him out of the foster care system, which is another issue entirely, but he didn't have to deal with his mom swooping in and overturning his entire life every three months."

Elena took a deep breath and set her knife down.

"Well, I didn't mean to tell you my whole life story," she laughed awkwardly. "I guess my brain trusts you more than I thought it did."

The corners of Cora's cheeks lifted, showing off her dimples. Her eyes remained fixed on her friend's. Elena took another deep breath and continued.

"Anyway, I want to help more kids do that. I want to help the kids who need homes to find them, and the ones that just need a way out of their own to find one, too. But I get too emotionally attached to be a social worker, so family law was the way to go for me."

Elena peeked at the other woman, and couldn't help but admire the soft blue eyes that hadn't strayed from her face.

"That's amazing, Elena. That was so awesome of your mom to do, and it clearly made a huge impact on you. I can't imagine how much better Everett's life must be now that his mom's not in it."

"Well." Elena smiled dryly. "This was 10 years ago now. He's got a wife and a house in Wilmington. He works for a pharmaceutical company out there. It's pretty cool. But, yeah."

She scratched the base of her skull with one finger, loosening the ponytail that held her hair back a little bit. "Anyway. That's what made me want to go to law school."

"Oh, oops! I thought it was more recent. That makes much more sense." Cora fair skin flushed, clearly feeling silly about the assumption she'd made. "Also, um, I think the stock is reduced? I'm not much of a cook, but this looks right."

Elena crossed the kitchen and looked into the pot, double-checking to make sure it was exactly right. "Yeah, you're right. Time to add the vegetables, potatoes, and the rest of the beef stock."

Walking back over, Elena picked up the bowl of vegetables and potatoes in one hand, and gestured toward the remainder of the box of stock with the other.

"Pour that in, and dinner will be in half an hour or so."

Cora grabbed the box and poured the rest of the stock in over the vegetables. Elena stirred everything around, and placed a lid on the dutch oven.

Turning around, Cora picked her phone up off the counter, and set a timer for thirty minutes.

"All right - time to relax!" Elena exclaimed. "We'll clean up after."

She walked around the counter to the living room, and let herself flop over the arm of the couch, somehow grabbing the blanket off of the back on the way down. She tucked the blanket around her and then turned so that her large frame was mostly covered by the fabric.

Cora laughed heartily at the sight

"That was smooth, Elena."

She unfurled herself from the blanket just far enough to stick her tongue out at her companion before whipping it back over her face.

Cora chose to plop into the wide, forest green armchair a few feet away. She curled her bare feet under her and nestled into the chair, squirming a little bit to get comfortable. Tilting her head back, she soaked in the comfortable silence of the apartment.

"How'd you get all this nice furniture?" Cora asked after a few minutes. Elena's apartment wasn't full of the Walmart and Ikea furniture that was so common in grad student apartments. "You're on the same shoestring budget as the rest of us grad students, aren't you?"

"All of this is either thrifted or an old family piece," Elena laughed lightly. "Mamá and my tías are all great at finding awesome stuff. They know what I like, so if they find something I can use, they'll send one of my brothers to go pick it up and bring it to me."

"I bet that turns out pretty badly on occasion. My Ma does that for me sometimes, but sometimes she picks things that are just strange." Cora turned in the chair, throwing her legs over the arm so she was looking directly at her Puerto Rican friend. "My mom once bought me these cat statues that are just…oh! Hang on. I think I have a picture."

She pulled her phone out again and began scrolling through pictures.

"They're just so creepy! Ha! Found them!" Passing the phone to Elena, she smiled in a way that was supposed to be evil, but was really just cute. "I used to take them to the lounge and leave them in weird places to creep out the other grad students. Then a janitor threatened to throw them away, so they're in my apartment's communal closet."

The gold-colored statues appeared to be two feet tall and looked like sinister Siamese cats, if they were mixed with giraffes. They were tall, slim, and looked like they had been carved out of a single piece of wood. Elena was pretty sure the necks of both of the cats were half the height of each statue.

"Those are… definitely creepy," Elena agreed. "As my Mamá would say, 'Así es el mambo' - that's how it goes when someone else is buying for you. Besides, it makes for a fun story, at least."

"It's definitely an icebreaker," Cora laughed and took her phone back. "You said you had aunts, though. How big is your family?"

"I'm the youngest of four siblings. Mamá is one of seven, and Papi is one of four. Papi's brothers still live in Puerto Rico, and three of Mamá's siblings do. The rest live here in the Triad."

Cora looked horrified.

"That's so much family. I can only imagine how much noise they'd make."

"Such is the life in a big family." Elena shook her head a little bit. "I didn't know anybody had anything different until like… middle school, maybe? It's pretty nice, but it can be really overwhelming. I think you'd like it, though."

Elena nodded, and thought back over her own family traditions for a moment before continuing.

"The only holiday we ever really do anything for is Christmas - it's Mamá's favorite, and there's a great tradition for Christmas Eve in Puerto Rico. Whenever one of my brothers moved out, we used to go and start singing carols at them in the middle of Christmas Eve, and then force them to feed us." Elena's amber eyes crinkled happily.

"We get together every holiday," Cora said. "But I've never heard of anything like that. That sounds like a lot more fun to me than any other kind of caroling!"

"It's fun the first few times," Elena admitted. "My brother Anton kept moving around, so we had to keep doing it for a few years. Sometimes a girl just wants to sleep on Christmas Eve, you know?"

"I feel that," Cora said, and fell silent for a few moments. "Do you have a bookshelf?"

"Yeah, it's right next to the bedroom. Why?" Elena asked, a little puzzled. "There isn't much on it."

"You learn a lot about a person from their bookshelf - no matter how small. Mind if I snoop?"

"Why ask?" Elena asked sarcastically, but not unkindly. Cora always gravitated towards books like a moth to a flame, only slightly less self-destructive. "You'll do it anyway."

"It's true, it's in my nature." Cora sighed dramatically. "I should have been a journalist, I guess. But seriously, okay by you to look?"

"Yeah, go for it. I'm gonna lay here till dinner's ready, though. I need to be quiet for a few minutes, so don't expect answers." Elena bundled herself up in the blanket, turning to face the back of the couch.

She could hear Cora lifting herself up from the armchair and padding across the room. Elena thought the avid reader would be disappointed by the shelf's minimal contents.

Elena thought that the middle shelf would probably hold more of Cora's attention. It held a few poetry books from authors like Sarah Kay and Gretchen Gomez, a gilded-edged bible that had been a First Communion gift from her grandfather, and a photo with her three brothers.

The bottom shelf held all of her textbooks tipped on their sides.

Elena was starting to worry about what Cora might be finding over there when Cora's phone started playing the Star Trek theme from her pocket - alerting her that the food should be done.

"It's time to eat!" Elena whooped and pulled herself

up from the couch. "Stop snooping through my stuff and let's eat!"

"ESTOY EMPACHADA," Elena breathed happily and set her food down. "God, I love food so much. People can call me fat all they want, but damn I love delicious food."

"That was amazing, Elena. Like, that was so good." Cora slid down in her chair so that her legs were straight out, with her heels touching the floor. Her teal tank top rode up, showing the stark white of her squishy, entirely untanned belly. "I'm 100 percent sure that that was better than anything in the world."

"Better than sex, huh?" Elena asked, glancing at her companion mischievously.

"Ha!" Cora barked a laugh. "Definitely better than sex for me. I'm asexual, and that's not really my thing."

"Oh cool. I didn't know. Are you sex-repulsed? I know some ace folks aren't." Elena asked.

"More sex-meh, if that makes sense?" Cora replied hesitantly. "It's okay, but I probably won't ever seek it out."

"Oh. I see." Elena thought for a moment. "Are you aromantic, too?"

"Nope." Cora smiled. "I'm panromantic. I love to date and romance everybody, I just don't have any interest in making love to anybody, ya know?"

Elena filed that away for later.

"That's cool. You know I'm a lesbian, right?"

"I feel like I knew that." Cora's eyes looked up and to the right, and Elena could tell she was trying to remember where she had learned this tidbit.

"I think you mentioned it the first time we talked about church?" she asked hesitantly.

Elena nodded.

"I remember now! You mentioned that a priest found out and was horrified, and your mom tore him a new one."

"Yep. It's unusual since I'm so blatantly queer, but Mamá is a badass," Elena grinned.

"I haven't even met her and I know she's a badass," Cora agreed.

"I'm surprised you remembered that. I try not to mention it around new people, and we haven't known each other that long. Church people and queer people don't usually mix.

"I don't usually tell people I'm ace unless it's necessary. I've had people drop me for it in the past," Cora admitted, tracing a figure eight on the table with her finger. "I feel like I can trust you not to judge me for it, though."

Elena reached across the table to her friend and placed a large, tawny brown hand on Cora's small, pale one.

"It's not an issue whatsoever." She smiled. "It shouldn't be for anyone who isn't an ass."

Cora's smile lit up her face, and she looked up at Elena again, her hand becoming still.

"Thanks, Elena. That means a lot."

"What are friends for?" Elena asked rhetorically. "I'd be a pretty shitty one if I did judge you for it."

"You'd be surprised," Cora said, her smile dimming a little. "I've been proven wrong before."

Elena grimaced.

"I'm sure you've got horror stories."

"Yeah, it's unfortunately common for ace, aro, bi and

trans folks to be shut out of their own communities because we weren't the "right" kind of queer," Cora said sadly. She took a deep breath and then widened her smile again a few heartbeats later. "Anyway, new topic. What's the plan for these dishes?"

"Yeah, yeah." Elena groaned, but pushed herself back from the table and stood up. "Also, you definitely owe me $20 cause I totally rocked your world with this soup."

"Deal," Cora laughed. "Next time I hit the ATM, it's yours! Or maybe I'll just buy you dinner next time."

"Now there's a deal I can get behind, as long as you help me with the dishes from this one."

Cora smiled and slid out of her chair.

Elena picked up both of the bowls on the table, and Cora picked up the silverware and napkins. Together they walked towards the kitchen in an easy silence to start cleaning up dinner. Both women smiled as they worked through the mess they'd made together.

Chapter 3

THE TWO WOMEN found themselves spending nearly every evening with each other, working together on their different class projects, or just getting dinner together when they couldn't work together.

Winter vacation would soon be upon them, which meant that they'd actually have time to themselves, once they got through exams.

"You will not believe it," Elena said huffily one early November afternoon as she walked through the door of Cora's apartment. Stepping through the door, she started unwrapping a thick wool scarf from around her neck. "I just got the worst news, Cora."

"Is everything okay?" Cora asked, her brows wrinkling in worry. "Your mom, your brothers? Is everyone all right?"

"Oh. Yeah, no, they're fine." Elena tossed the scarf and coat on the rack by the door. Elena walked over to the bed and flopped onto it dramatically. "Not exactly the worst news, I guess, but even you'll admit that it's pretty terrible. My tías are coming to visit for Christmas!"

"Oh, that'll be fun, right?" Cora asked confusedly. "It'll be nice to have your family for Christmas! That's what Christmas is for, right?"

"Yeah," Elena groaned. "But they're gonna be here next week! And they're staying until New Years! They'll be here forever, Cora. Forever."

She covered her face with one of Cora's pillows and screamed quietly into it.

"Oh god." Cora grimaced. "That is a really long time for them to visit with no warning."

Elena pulled the pillow down so her glaring brown eyes were visible over the top.

"You have no idea. There are five of them," she said in a quiet, anguished voice. "They each come up with their husbands, and at least three suitcases each. Every one of those will then be filled with thrift store finds, and food that's really expensive in Puerto Rico. They take it to my Abuela, who still lives there. They are also bringing all of my cousins - all eleven of them!

"And two of them are staying with me," she whined pitifully. "My living room has been co-opted so Camila and Adriana can stay somewhere together."

"That's also what you get for having so much space to yourself," Cora said unsympathetically. "At least I have the excuse of roommates to get out of hosting my family."

"You don't get it, Cora," Elena huffed from behind the pillow. "Camila and Adriana are the oldest ones. They're 17-year-old twins who barely talk to anyone other than themselves. It's creepy."

Cora grimaced in agreement.

"Okay, that would be weird. I'm with you now."

Cora sat on the queen sized bed facing Elena where she lay, face still hidden under the pillow. Cora crossed her legs underneath her and tugged the pillow away from her friend's face.

Elena grimaced as she realized there was a maroon lipstick print on the pillowcase where she'd used it as a scream silencer, but Cora didn't notice.

"C'mere, you."

Cora put the pillow on her lap and patted it for Elena to put her head on. Elena obliged, shifting herself sideways and pulling her knees up so her feet were flat on the soft floral comforter that covered the bed.

"How can I help?" Cora asked, pulling stray hairs away from Elena's forehead and smoothing her dark, curly hair against the pillow. "What can I do to make it easier?"

"Make my cousins miraculously decide not to visit?" Elena asked hopefully, her full lips pouting at Cora.

"I flunked mind reading and control in undergrad. Sorry, love." Cora smiled ruefully down at her friend.

"Mierda!" Elena exclaimed with a laugh. "You are no use to me!"

"It's not like you passed, either!" Cora shot back jokingly. "Seriously, though, can I help at all? At the very least, you can always call me and rant. Or come over and rant. Whichever works."

"I'll think about it," Elena said. "At least they gave us two week's notice that they were coming this time. Once when I was little, they showed up completely unannounced and were surprised when no one picked them up from the airport!"

"Wow. That's something."

Cora realized she was still petting her friend's head and pulled her hand back. She fidgeted with her earrings to give her hands something else to do, and in a failed attempt to hide the flush on her face.

"Seriously, if there's anything I can do to help, I'm more than willing. I'm used to my tiny Methodist family. How different can your big old Catholic family be?"

Elena laughed until tears leaked down her chubby cheeks

"Oh, sweetie. You have no idea."

DIVING BACK INTO THEIR STUDIES, Cora and Elena bundled up in the library working on their end of semester projects throughout the next few weeks. Doctor Burgess had assigned an extensive case law review for each student, focusing on a specific issue in each of their fields. Elena had chosen HIPAA, and Cora had chosen trademark law, focusing on book title trademarking practices.

So far, Cora was pretty convinced she'd picked the more interesting topic. There was a very recent case that summed up a lot of issues with trademarking specific words - in this case, the word cocky. It made for some interesting doodles in the margins of her notes, for sure.

No matter which topic was more interesting, neither of them were getting much work done between sneaking furtive glances at each other from across the table and "accidentally" brushing their fingers against each other as they reached for the books they wanted to work from.

Cora knew she'd never get the 30-page review done at this pace. She had just enough of it done to make it so that she didn't absolutely have to focus on it right now, so of course, she wasn't focused at all. She could hear the shuffle of feet around the corner from their table and kept looking even though she knew that whoever was there didn't matter. There was just enough sound in the alcove to distract her, but she didn't want to put on her headphones in case Elena needed her for something.

She watched Elena mouth the words she was reading as she copied them onto her laptop. She leaned forward, holding her long hair out of her face with one hand, while she typed with the other. Her round face was puckered in focus, deep wrinkles forming in her normally smooth forehead, and Cora couldn't rip her gaze away.

After a few moments, Elena looked up and caught Cora's gaze. Her chubby golden cheeks turned distinctly pink. Cora felt her own heat as well at getting caught staring, but Elena's plump lips turned upwards into a smile.

"Like what you see?"

Cora stammered, feeling her whole face turn red. She hid her face in her hands, peeking out when Elena let loose a peal of laughter that reminded her of handbells.

As she peered across the table, she realized that something had changed outside the window behind Elena. Where there had been a slate gray sky, soft, white flakes drifted down, forming a slush on the ground. She gasped and jumped up from the table.

Elena started.

"What's wrong?" She asked, automatically assuming the worst.

"Elena, it's snowing! It's December 4th and it's actually snowing!" She sounded like a little kid and knew that her voice was much too high and loud for the law library's standards, but at that moment she didn't care.

The other woman let out a gasp of her own and

whirled to look out the window. Cora could see the reflection of her wide brown eyes in the glass of the window.

Snow was rare in North Carolina winters. Both women were much more used to ice - snow's more treacherous companion.

"Oh, let's go play in it. Quick, pack up your things!" They could hear others in the library making the same realization they had. "Before the rest of them squash the fresh snow!"

Cora scrambled to follow her instructions, carefully placing the law books onto the cart next to their table for replacement on the shelves. She snapped a picture of their Dewey Decimal codes for easy memory for whenever they came back.

"No, no, you can leave the books. We can come back once we've been outside for a few minutes. Just put your laptop and things away so no one swipes them," Elena told her, tossing her own things into a bag and hiding them between the stacks of books on the table.

"Oh, smart!" Cora followed suit, double checking to make sure their bags weren't visible to general passersby. When they were both satisfied, they started to dress.

In an echo of one of their earlier trips, they power walked to the main doors of the library, pulling their coats, hats, and gloves on as they went. They weren't the only ones doing it.

I bet Elena looks beautiful in the snow, Cora thought to herself, beginning to blush anew at the thought. She knew it was silly even as she thought it. Elena was beautiful no matter the weather.

The other students' faces were as bright as Elena's was as she turned back to where Cora stood.

"Well, come on! You don't want to miss what might be our only snowstorm this year!"

Elena held out a dainty gloved hand, and Cora took it with a grin.

"Let's go be snow angels."

THEY BURST through the double doors into the crisp wintry air. The snow was already sticking to the grass and trees, thanks to almost three weeks of below freezing temperatures. It was beautiful.

Cora turned to look at Elena and found her with her face turned towards the grey sky. Her flat-tipped nose was tinged pink from the cold, and her eyes were closed. A serene smile spread across her golden brown face. It was so peaceful that Cora's heart skipped a beat looking at her.

"I didn't know you liked the snow," she remarked once she caught her breath.

"Nobody with any sense of joy doesn't like snow," Elena replied without opening her eyes. She turned her face toward Cora and her smile widened. "Have you caught a snowflake on your tongue yet?"

"Not yet! But I haven't really tried either. I've been watching you."

Elena opened her eyes and they were twinkling in the snow.

"Creep!"

She stuck her tongue out at the shorter girl, and almost instantly caught a flake on her tongue. Cora giggled and echoed the movement, spinning a little where she stood.

Several cold flakes hit her tongue, melting instantly.

She opened her own eyes to find Elena with her phone out catching the moment on video.

"Now who's the creep?" Elena just laughed her deep belly laugh.

"I'm sorry, I couldn't resist. You were too pretty in the snow, especially in that bright red coat. Can I post this on Insta?"

Cora rolled her eyes.

"Am I cute in it?"

"You're always cute."

"Then yes, you can post it on Insta and tag me in it," Cora acquiesced. "As long as you let me get one of you."

"Do y'all want me to get a picture of you two together?"

They both turned, to find a heavy, dark-skinned Black woman looking at them expectantly, with a large camera in hand.

"You mean us?" Cora asked.

"Yeah. Y'all are real cute! Plus I work for The Carolinian, and we wanted to get some snow pictures for this week's edition."

They exchanged glances and shrugged.

"Go for it! Do you want us to do anything in particular?"

The woman shrugged and shifted her camera to her eye.

"I thought the dancing you were doing was really pretty. We don't do posed shots, but if y'all wanted to dance in the snow, I wouldn't say no to the pictures."

Cora fidgeted nervously and Elena flashed the photographer a grin, holding out a hand to Cora.

"My lady?"

Cora took her hand with a small giggle, and Elena wrapped her up in her arms.

"Is this okay?" she whispered. Cora nodded.

"This is good. I'm not cold anymore!" Elena started to waltz, counting to three steps before turning, with Cora in step.

"You wouldn't be cold if you were wearing a hat, you know."

Cora wrinkled her nose at Elena, smiling at the same time. She could hear the reporter's camera taking pictures rapidly behind them.

"Hats make my hair not cute, and also make me look like a two-year-old. I do not want to look like an ugly two-year-old!"

Elena laughed, tilting her head back slightly.

"No one would ever mistake you for an ugly two-year-old, Cora. Can I twirl you?"

Cora felt the heat rise to her cheeks, tinting them red in a way that had nothing to do with the cold. She nodded again, and Elena twirled her around in the snow. It was like there was nothing around them but thick, swirling snowflakes.

Cora had to resist the urge to kiss her as she went under the taller woman's arm. No way was she going to do that for the first time without permission, let alone in front of a newspaper photographer. As she wrapped her arm back around Elena's waist, bringing them closer together, the photographer stopped taking pictures and interrupted them.

"Oh, my god. You two are just the cutest couple I've ever seen," the photographer said. "I think I've got plenty of pictures, and I don't want to interrupt, but I wanted to get your numbers so I could send you some of these."

Glancing at Elena, Cora dropped her arm from her waist and turned towards the Black woman. She didn't separate herself from where she leaned against Elena's stomach and chest. She pulled her phone out of her coat pocket and handed it to the photographer. Elena looked over the top of her head at the photographer

"Oh, I really want these pictures. Punch your number in and I'll text you. I can get them to Elena."

The photographer did as she was told and handed the phone back before sliding her camera into her purse.

"Thanks so much, really. Y'all really are just adorable together. It'll make a great centerpiece on the front page!"

She sauntered off without waiting for a response, and they both looked at each other askance.

"Front page?" they said together.

"Well, I guess that'll be a nice way to come out to the entire school. Good thing we weren't hiding it before?"

"I guess so! Plus, how many people actually read the campus newspaper anyway?"

"It can't be that many," Elena decided. "You ready to go inside?"

"Yeah, I guess. We do need to finish our case reviews," Cora sighed. Elena wrapped an arm around her shoulders, and they walked back into the building together.

Chapter 4

THE NEXT WEEK, the brass of the theme song from
The Incredibles blasted from Cora's phone, making her
jump. She ran over to her desk and started tossing the
Diet Coke cans that had been strewn across its surface
into her wire trash can. The desk didn't look big enough
to lose anything on, but her messiness had proved it was
possible.

"I need you to come over." Elena's deep voice
sounded panicked as soon as Cora unearthed the phone
from the desk in her apartment. "I need you to bring the
ice cream drumsticks, coconut milk, cream of coconut,
evaporated milk and sweetened condensed milk. Oh!
And rum!"

"That's a weird combination, but okay," Cora took
the order in stride, but stood from where she sat. "I got
questions."

"That's fine, cause I've got answers."

"Let me get a pen," Cora said, barely covering a
laugh.

"What flavor ice cream for the drumsticks? Do you

49

have a preference for a brand of coconut milk? How much of each?"

Cora rummaged in the canvas tote she used as a purse until she found her reporter's notebook and a pink rollerball pen.

"Okay, I'm set. Starting with the ice cream?"

"One box of drumsticks, just the vanilla dipped in chocolate will be perfect." Cora could tell that with each word she spoke, Elena was calming down a little bit. Her voice softened as she listed the items. "You'll find all of the other ingredients in the international foods section - Goya's the brand you want. You ready for amounts?"

"I am…now," Cora said hurriedly, her pen at the ready knowing she would need to write fast.

"Okay - four twelve-ounce cans of evaporated milk; two fifteen-ounce cans of cream of coconut; two cans of coconut milk, I think like thirteen-ounce cans?; and then one can of sweetened condensed milk. You got all that?" Elena paused between each item as if she knew that Cora couldn't write as fast as she could speak, especially while holding her phone in her other hand.

Cora read back the list item by item, waiting for her friend's sí of confirmation before she moved on.

"Okay, and I'm guessing white rum? Do you need a flavored rum?"

"Nope, just plain old white rum. It doesn't even need to be expensive," Elena's voice sounded like she was incredibly overwhelmed, though she was calmer than when the conversation first started, which was a relief for Cora. "Just bring me the rum, please!"

"Aye, aye, captain," Cora clicked the pen closed and tossed it in her purse."I'll be there in 45 minutes, and will call you if there are any issues. Good?"

"God bless you and get you here as fast as possible. Door's unlocked, just let yourself in. I gotta go! Bye!"

The phone beeped to say the call had ended and Cora blinked at it, still a little confused about what she'd find when she reached her friend's apartment. Shaking her head, she grabbed her purse and keys and walked out into the common room.

After shutting and locking her door, she pulled the dry erase marker out of its wall bracket and scribbled a note on the whiteboard that hung on the door

Headed to Elena's. Be back tomorrow — CM

CORA WHIPPED into the parking lot, having sped from the grocery store to the apartment complex to bring the emergency groceries to her friend.

She had no idea what the emergency was, or why Elena needed all of this stuff, but Elena wasn't unreasonable ninety percent of the time. She wouldn't have called in a panic if she didn't need it.

Getting out of the car, Cora shot her friend a text that simply said "Here" and popped open the trunk of her shiny green hatchback. She grabbed the three bags and slung them over one arm. She bumped the trunk shut with her hip, slipped her phone into her back pocket and transferred one of the bags to her other arm.

She walked through the complex's breezeway to Elena's ground floor apartment and found the heavy bass music of a pop song blaring from the normally near-silent apartment. Twisting the handle of the unlocked door open, she slid into the apartment unnoticed.

Four people were dancing around Elena's normally

spotless living room. The lights were off, and the lamps seemed to have been replaced with strobe lights, which showed that the furniture had been pushed up against the walls.

It turned the living room into a club scene. Elena would have hated it if she'd been in the room.

Cora took a second glance around the room. Elena definitely wasn't in the room, but she could see where someone's iPhone was plugged into an auxiliary cord on the counter. She walked over and set the bags on the ground. Picking up the phone, she paused the music. It took the dancers a second to notice what had happened.

"¡Oye! ¿Porqué apagaste la música?" The tallest one screeched. Cora couldn't make out any defining features on any of them in the pulsing light of the room. It was making her head swim.

"Someone turn off the strobe lights before you give me a stroke," she commanded, and one of the dancers scrambled to do as they were told. The room plunged into darkness. "That's better. Now where the hell is Elena?"

"Back here!" She heard a yell that made her jump in the otherwise silent room and startled all of the others judging by the surprise on their faces. "I'm not coming out! Can you put the ice cream in the freezer?"

"Uh... Okay?" Cora said with confusion. The four started whispering to each other where they'd returned to huddle in the middle of the room. She slid the ice cream into the freezer and put everything else in the fridge for good measure.

"Can we turn the music back on now?" One of them asked in a whiny tone that was the perfect stereotype for a teenage girl.

"No! Is this your house?!" Cora asked, squinting at

them, and flipping on the kitchen lights. "I know Elena didn't give you permission for this if she's hiding in her bedroom in her own apartment."

The four people in shorts and crop tops blinked guiltily at each other.

"I thought so. Put this room back together and act like your mothers raised you right," she said disapprovingly. The four leggy creatures in the middle of the room sprung to Cora's command as she stalked towards Elena's bedroom.

"Are they still out there?" Elena asked quietly when Cora slid the door shut behind her. Cora had never seen a look of panic on her face like this.

Cora nodded, and Elena visibly deflated. "I hoped they'd leave when you got here."

Elena tipped forward from where she sat on her bed, face planting onto it with a groan that sounded remarkably like "I hate teenagers."

"I take it those are your cousins?" Cora asked, getting what she thought was a nod in response. "I thought you only had two of them staying with you."

Elena lifted her head slightly and mournfully replied, "They brought friends." She then let her head drop back into the grey pin-tucked comforter.

"Okay, well your cousins and their friends are putting your living room back together now," Cora said softly, sitting down beside her friend on the bed. "Now, what can we do for you?"

"Wanna help me make really rummy coquitos?" Elena said, a slight whine to her voice that made Cora's heart stutter a little.

"Sure thing, honey." Cora smiled. Standing, she held a hand out to her friend, who took it with a tired smile of her own. "But first we have to get rid of the teenagers.

Call your mom and see if she can take them for the evening before I murder them since you're not in any kind of shape to get rid of them."

A few minutes later, the women walked into the living room together, lightly holding hands, to find the teenagers pushing the last armchair back into place.

"Oh, ¿esa es tu novia?" The tallest girl said in a surprised voice. Elena and Cora looked at each other with a startled expression, and simultaneously let go of each other's hand.

"I'm not her girlfriend," Cora said quickly, hoping they didn't notice the blush on her face. "Just a good friend. And I'm glad y'all put this room back together so quickly."

"We only shoved it off to the side so we could dance," one of the other girls mumbled. "It's not like we threw a rager in here."

"Who throws a party at someone else's house without permission?" Cora glared at the girl, and she shut up immediately. "You've stressed Elena out so bad she was hiding in her room, and that's not okay. You all owe her an apology before her mother comes to pick y'all up. You hear me?"

"Tía Maria is coming? Why?" The girl looked genuinely confused, and Elena rolled her eyes before walking back into her bedroom and shutting the door, muttering to herself.

"You're her cousins, you should know she hates loud music. I've known her for three months and I could have told you that," Cora snapped and shook her head. "You are her guests and you took over her living room. Now, which two of you are cousins, and which are friends?"

The tall girl who had mostly spoken in Spanish thus far glared at her, but answered after a moment.

"I'm Adriana, and the one in pink is Camila." Adriana pointed at the girl closest to the wall, who gave Cora a small wave. "And these are our friends Jennifer and Katie. They live here."

The two girls in the middle glanced between Cora and Adriana, clearly confused as to what was going on.

"Um, is your aunt picking us up, too, Adri?" The one Adriana had pointed out as Katie said hesitantly. "Cause, um, we can just go? Jen drove."

"No, you don't want to go to Tía's house. It's boring." Adriana rolled her eyes, then stopped and glanced at her sister. "I mean, you can if you want. There's nothing to do there, either."

Camila gave her sister a small smile, and Adriana relaxed a little bit. Cora could tell that Camila was more like Elena than Adriana, from her slightly anxious body language.

"Nah, we'll go. We'll hook up tomorrow, okay?" Jennifer looked like there was nothing she'd like better than to run away, and she intended to do just that. Cora couldn't keep herself from smiling wickedly as she realized how uncomfortable everyone in this apartment was.

Good, she thought. Be uncomfortable, like you made Elena, you little jerks.

Jennifer and Katie made their way out as quickly as possible. A few moments passed where the girls all stared at one another, seeming too awkward to say anything out loud. Then a loud knocking sounded through the apartment, and the front door swung open.

A woman who matched Elena from head to toe swept in. Unlike Elena, this woman kept her dark hair short in a cloud around her head and wore a black maxi dress that Elena would have looked stunning in. Cora recognized her instantly as Elena's mother.

Maria Mendez had a presence that could not be hidden. Between her towering stance and the glare in her eyes, no one could have hidden from her at that moment. Even bold Adriana wilted before her aunt's fierce glare.

The heavyset woman lit into them in Spanish, speaking too quickly for Cora to keep up. They gathered up their things and walked out the open door that Maria was pointing to. Maria waved at Cora, and then nearly sprinted out after them, leaving the door open.

"Thank God they're gone," Elena breathed as she shut the door and locked it behind her cousins. She muttered what sounded like a prayer under her breath before she turned away from it to find Cora sitting on the counter next to the stove with a bottle of rum the size of her head in her lap.

"Amen to that. Now, what's this bottle of rum for?" Cora grinned evilly, and Elena couldn't help but grin back.

"IT'S NOT for drinking straight, you heathen!" Elena laughed and took the large bottle from her friend. That's how you destroy your liver."

Cora slid off the counter and hopped over to the fridge where she had stashed all of the coconut products.

She laughed as she noticed that Elena had a copy of The Carolinian on the fridge that showed them twirling together. She had to admit it was a good picture, but it hadn't gotten nearly as much attention from their classmates as they'd expected it to.

"So what are we making?" Cora asked as she pulled everything she'd bought out. "This looks like it could make eggnog if it was coconut flavored."

"You're not wrong," Elena admitted as she pulled out her blender. "It's basically coconut eggnog - which is much more delicious than regular eggnog. We call it coquito, and tonight, we're making it strong."

"Hell yeah!" Cora exclaimed. "First, did I get everything right from the store? I don't wanna mess it up."

Elena turned to look at what Cora had bought and nodded at each item.

"Looks like all we need from the cupboard is cinnamon, vanilla extract…" She dove into the cabinet where she kept her spices, pulling out the items she'd named. "And the good glasses. Can you grab those?"

Cora walked over to the cabinet she'd pointed to. Looking for the glasses with the weighted bottoms that she knew Elena was talking about, she started to laugh. Elena looked over at her and joined her laughing. There was no way Cora, who was just over five feet tall, could reach the glasses off of the top shelf of the cupboard.

"Well, all right then, shorty," Elena grinned at her friend, who had stopped laughing and was now pouting playfully. "I guess I'll grab those."

"If only I had orangutan arms like my brothers!" Cora lamented dramatically. "Alas, I have wimpy girl arms that are the right length for my body. This is my fatal flaw."

"Orangutan arms?" Elena said, sounding bemused. "You just pulled that phrase out of your ass? You can use your 'wimpy girl arms' to open up all the cans. The can opener is in the thing."

Cora pouted at her for a moment longer, then

walked over and did as she was told, as she had learned was the best option in the kitchen. Elena brought the pint-sized glasses over to where they had everything set up and looked over the ingredients.

"Okay, we're ready to go." She nodded. "Half of everything goes in the blender, except the rum."

"Wait, you mean we aren't getting drunk off our asses?" Cora asked, a teasing note in her voice.

"Not that drunk," Elena clarified. "I'd like to survive the night, so we're not putting a half gallon of rum in a gallon of coquito. We'd die if we did."

"Fair enough, even if that's a little bit of quitter talk." Cora shrugged and started dumping the various cans of coconut product into the blender. Elena measured out and dumped a tablespoon of vanilla and a half tablespoon of cinnamon into the mixture.

"Isn't it funny-" Cora was cut off by the sound of the blender whirring to life and waited for it to finish combining the mixture into what would be coquito. When it was done blending, Elena turned it off.

"I'm sorry, what were you saying?" She asked, bustling to get the mixture into the four glasses on the counter.

"I was saying, wasn't it funny that Adriana thought we were dating?" Cora asked with a smile. Elena's back was to her, but Cora thought she saw it stiffen ever so slightly, and she began to backpedal. "Not that I wouldn't date you, I mean - wow that came out really wrong. Hang on."

Taking a deep breath, Cora tried again.

"I guess I didn't expect your family to be so cool about it?" Cora said, though Elena still wasn't looking at her. "My cousins are mostly the "we'll ignore it and pretend we're okay till we have to deal with it" type of Methodists. I figured yours would be the same."

Elena turned around, and her face was tighter than it had been but not as bad as Cora feared it would be.

"Grab two cups and stick them in the fridge," she commanded, and Cora obeyed. "My family's mostly okay with it. They're not as religious as my abuela was. My cousins are more accepting of me being a lesbian than my tía's, mostly - I think it's a generational thing."

"Oh, and I guess we did walk out of your bedroom holding hands. I suppose it isn't the weirdest assumption to make."

"Yeah…" Elena said as she watched Cora's face from the corner of her eye. "I also kind of told them about you."

"Oh? What did you tell them about me?" Cora raised an eyebrow. "Good things I hope?"

"I'll tell you after we've had a few drinks," Elena said with a dramatic wink. "Help me clean up, wouldja?"

"You're not mad, right?" Cora said worriedly, but still grabbing a can to toss into the garbage. "I didn't upset you? You seemed a little upset."

"Nah," Elena smiled, and her posture was as relaxed as it had been all night. "We're all good."

Cora smiled back. The two girls cleaned the kitchen together in companionable silence, each feeling that everything was just right, waiting for the coquito to be cold enough to drink.

THEY STOOD TOGETHER UNTIL, seemingly out of nowhere, Elena gasped and dove toward the freezer.

Cora jumped a little where she stood leaning against the counter.

"You okay, El?" she asked worriedly.

"I just remembered you bought drumsticks!" Elena exclaimed happily. "Yessss! I'm so happy."

Cora watched, her shock melting into a soft smile as Elena did a happy dance.

"I didn't know you liked these so much," Cora said with a smile. Elena handed her one of the packages and began to unwrap her own with relish.

"Mamá would always let us have these as a treat after church on Sundays, and then on really bad days, to cheer us up," Elena explained, tossing the plastic wrapper in the trash. "They are my very favorite comfort food in the world."

Cora unwrapped her own as well. Elena took a big bite of the nut- and chocolate-dipped vanilla ice cream cone and moaned.

"This is exactly what I needed. God, that makes almost everything better. What it can't fix, I know the coquito can! It should be cool enough to drink now. Grab a glass and a spoon and stir it up!"

She followed her own instructions with delight and wandered over to her couch, which was more or less where it had been before the Puerto Rican twin monstrosities had shown up. Both women settled into opposite ends of the couch, their feet almost touching at the couch's seams.

Elena took a long sip and sighed.

"Sweet merciful silence, how I love thee," she said reverently. Cora smiled at the darker skinned woman over her own drink. "I love the quiet. I get so little of it, between classes and studying."

"And me," Cora pointed out. "I've always got music playing."

Elena waved her hand and shook her head.

"I'd put up with more than just music playing to spend time with you. You're worth it to me." Becoming abruptly less serious, she squinted across the couch and added, "For now."

"For now, huh?" Cora laughed. "What, does my friendship expire after Christmas?"

"Don't be silly!" Elena lightly nudged her friend with her foot, her face looking slightly tense. "You aren't getting rid of me yet. I was actually about to invite you to the family Christmas party?"

Elena's voice lilted up at the end, making it a question.

"Of course I'll come to your Christmas party, you nerd." Cora laughed and nudged her friend back. Elena's mouth twisted into a small smile, and her face relaxed around it. "How else would I find out what you told your family about me?"

"I should have known not to tell you that." Elena rolled her eyes. "You're gonna be thinking about that for weeks, aren't you?"

"Unless you tell me what you told them!" Cora batted her eyelashes at Elena with a laugh that wrinkled her nose.

"I swear it was all nice stuff," she said once Cora's giggles had subsided. "I told them about your plans to write a book, and how you're working your way through school by freelancing. I may have also told them you're adorable and distractible as fuck."

Cora froze. A moment later, she asked in a soft voice "Did you tell them I was ADHD?"

Her voice may have been soft, but her eyes were

hard, and somehow pleading. "I mean, it's not a bad thing, but I don't usually tell people that until they've known me a while?"

Elena cocked her head and took a slurp of her coquito, swallowing before she answered.

"You told me the first day we studied in the library that you were ADHD, Cora. I didn't think it would be a problem since I told them a lot of other things about you." She moved her legs off the couch and sat up straight, her body still turned towards Cora.

"Sorry." Cora rubbed the bridge of her nose, clearly calming herself down. "I'm not mad. It's okay. People just have a bad reaction a lot when I tell them I'm ADHD. I usually hide it unless I absolutely have to say something, and just… I don't know, let them think I'm not listening to them 'cause they're boring."

"I'm sorry, Cora. I should have asked you before I said anything to them," Elena's face wrinkled apologetically, and she spoke softly. "I didn't want them to meet you and be surprised and be accidental douchebags, you know. My family's pretty cool about most things, but learning disabilities are things they can be weird about when they don't know about it."

Elena rolled her glass of coquito, nearly empty now, between her hands, not looking at Cora. She hated that she'd made her upset, and was mad at herself for it.

"I like you, Cora." Her voice dropped to a whisper. "I really like you. I want them to like you almost as much as I do. I'm sorry I didn't ask first."

Cora set her glass on the end table next to her and maneuvered her body so that she was sitting parallel to Elena, who still wasn't meeting her eyes. She scooted closer and wrapped an arm around Elena's warm, broad shoulders.

"Hey," Cora whispered, using her free hand to move Elena's hair away from her face. "It's okay. I'm not mad. I do wish you'd asked first, but you didn't, and we'll deal with it. They'd have found out eventually if this goes where I think it's going. If it helps, I really like you, too, Elena."

Hearing Cora say that she really liked her warmed Elena through, despite the chill of the coquito in her hand.

Elena finally looked sideways at Cora and smiled a tight-lipped smile.

"That does help," Elena said. "I'm still sorry, though."

"That's why it's okay." Cora smiled back. "Now come hug me, you mess."

And so she did.

—————————————————————

Chapter 5

—————————————————————

ON THE AFTERNOON of the party, Elena had planned to meet Cora at the three bedroom apartment she shared with her roommates. Elena had rid herself of her own temporary roommates again, having pawned them off on her mother so they could help prepare for the party.

Cora's roommates, Jacqueline and Ebony, were rarely home - they preferred to spend their time at their boyfriends' houses when they weren't cramming like the rest of the college students. That was not the case this afternoon, though.

Elena could hear them talking before she knocked on the door. Rapping three times, they quieted and Ebony answered the door.

"Oh hey, girl! How's it goin'?" she asked with a smile, her teeth bright against her olive-toned brown skin.

"Hey! Nice to see you, Ebony!" Elena smiled back. "It's going pretty well - I'm here to help Cora get ready for the family Christmas party! How've you been?"

"I've been good! Ready for this stressful as hell semester to be over, that's for sure." Ebony sighed.

"Amen to that," Elena exclaimed. "I'm tired of doing all this mess."

"I feel you," Ebony agreed. "Though, you're the one who picked law school. You had to expect at least a little bit of this."

"So says the med student!" Cora poked her head out of her bedroom door and piped in with a laugh. "Both of y'all are overachievers."

Elena and Ebony looked at each other and nodded.

"Worth it," Ebony shrugged and began to walk back to where Jacqueline sat watching tv in the living room, her natural cloud of hair bouncing with every step. Elena and Jacqueline had never really gotten to know each other. Jacqueline, though another Latina, didn't seem at all inclined to change that, so Elena shrugged it off.

"C'mon, Elena." Cora gestured to her. "I have no idea what to wear to a Puerto Rican Christmas party."

"I think I can help with that," Elena said with a mischievous smile. "It's weirdly formal."

ELENA AND CORA arrived at Elena's mother's house several hours later, wearing beautiful dresses of different styles.

Cora's was an emerald green satin A-line dress that suited her pale coloring. The cut of the dress flattered her willowy figure. A pale golden mesh and a pair of matching sequined flats glittered, bookending the outfit. Elena wore a burgundy wrap gown that accentuated her many curves and complimented her warm skin tone.

"I look okay, right?" Cora asked nervously, patting the sides of her hair. She had puffed her blonde curls up a little bit and put mousse in them to keep them where she wanted them.

Cora noticed that Elena hadn't styled her dark, curly hair into an updo for once - she'd chosen to lean into her natural waves, and had used a decorative comb to sweep all of her hair to one side.

"Don't be silly, Cor," Elena laughed. "You look fantastic. They're all gonna love you."

"Except your cousins," Cora muttered, her cheeks warming at the nickname. "They probably told everyone how bitchy I am."

"Eh." Elena waved off the concern. "They know I like you, and they like me better than Adriana, at least. Camila is sweet when she can get out from under Adri's shadow. You'll see."

"If you say so."

She could see that Cora was still chewing on the inside of her lip.

"I do say so," Elena said decisively and held out her hand. Cora took it with a grateful smile, and they walked up the driveway together towards Elena's mother's house.

Before they reached the door, it swung open, pouring light, sound, and warmth into the cold, dark evening.

"Welcome!" A tall, stocky man exclaimed from the doorway. "Elena! It is so good to see you, mi vida!"

After stepping onto the porch, Elena dropped Cora's hand to hug the man.

"Papi, it's good to see you too! They have you on door duty this year?"

"Ay, it was my turn, sadly." He shrugged, but still smiled a wide smile that reminded Cora of Elena's. "But it means I get to see you first, and meet your lovely friend!"

"Hi," Cora ventured nervously, sticking her hand out for a handshake. "I'm Cora."

Elena's father grabbed her hand and pulled her in for a tight hug. His large arms wrapped around her waist.

"Merry Christmas, Cora!" He exclaimed, using his arms to swing her through the door to the party that awaited.

THE LARGE HOME Cora found herself in was awash with Christmas decorations in a way that was almost overwhelming. From their first step inside the door, Cora and Elena could see two full-sized Christmas trees, and garlands with lights and ornaments hung throughout the room. Cora was stunned at the beauty of the decorations.

As she took a few more steps into the room, she noticed there was a village and a running train underneath the Christmas tree that could be seen by the window. She could feel her jaw drop. It was all so beautiful.

"This is your Christmas party every year?" Cora whispered in astonishment as Elena stepped up beside her. "I wish I could paint this, but no one would believe it."

Elena was grinning. Cora could see her tongue where it was sitting between her teeth. It was adorable.

"Welcome to the Mendez version of Christmas, Cora," Elena announced. "Come meet the family!"

As if Elena had summoned her family, Cora was immediately surrounded, with each of them introducing themselves in a blur. She recognized a few of the men from the pictures in Elena's apartment, and she spotted the twins standing off to the side of the room texting.

"Don't worry — there's no test later," Elena's eldest brother Anton joked. At least she thought it was a joke. Cora felt relieved anyway. There were just way too many people for her to remember all of their names, especially with the sensory overload that this room was even without them in it. It was like being in a human, Christmas-scented whirlwind.

One of the children had become glued to Elena within a half-hour of their arrival. Her oldest niece, Sofía, was attached to her hip. Literally. The sight of the girl sitting on Elena's hip, her head on her shoulder, made Cora's heart ache in a way she couldn't quite explain.

Sofía informed Cora that she was four years old — and Elena's favorite. The beaming smile on Elena's face said that this wasn't untrue. Elena was happy here, surrounded by her family.

"Sofía, can you go hang out with your Papa?" Elena asked sweetly while setting the girl down. "Cora hasn't met your Grandmamá yet, and she'll get very offended if we don't go say hey soon."

"Okay, but as soon as Grandmamá is done, come find me, okay?" Sofía didn't wait for an answer, scampering off towards the rest of the house. Elena turned her thousand watt smile to Cora.

"You ready?"

Cora ran her fingers along the seam of her dress, adjusting her shrug so it looked just right. She was more than a little intimidated by the woman she'd met while herding teenagers out of Elena's apartment.

"Okay." She nodded. "I think I'm ready to meet your mother for real."

Taking a deep breath, she held out her hand to Elena, who was completely relaxed despite the crowds and the noise. Elena took it and deftly led her to the kitchen.

Elena's mother stood in the middle of the kitchen wielding a spatula like a scepter. The fat, elegant woman was wearing a "What's Cooking, Good Looking?" apron over a sapphire blue gown. The entire room revolved around her.

Then she turned around and locked eyes with Cora. It felt to Cora like everyone in the room slammed to a halt to stare at her as well, but really they'd just glanced her way and gone back to whatever they were doing.

María's skin was darker and more wrinkled than her daughter's, but her eyes were the same honeyed brown. They were as full of warmth and care as Elena's as well.

"You must be Cora! I'm María, but you may also call me Mama," she proclaimed in a thicker Puerto Rican accent than Elena's, but a warmer voice than the last time they'd met. "Welcome to our home!"

She untied the apron from around her and hung it on the nearest cabinet doorknob. The next thing Cora knew, she was wrapped up in a hug that smelled like all of Christmas in one human, with a hint of floral perfume.

"Thank you for all you do for my girl," she whispered in Cora's ear. "She needed a friend like you."

"I needed a friend like her, too," Cora whispered back with eyes that were suddenly threatening to spill tears. "She is truly a gift."

María pulled her head back and released Cora from her embrace after taking a long look at the pale girl's face. She then turned the full force of her attention on her daughter.

"Have you eaten yet, my love?" she demanded, rather than asked. "I worry about you all alone in that apartment with no one to make you eat properly."

"Mama, I live half an hour away from you. I'm hardly all alone." Elena rolled her eyes, but her mouth showed the love with a wide smile. "But I will definitely eat."

María raised a hand to say something else, but Elena cut her off with raised eyebrows.

"And I will take leftovers home. But right now, the real dinner isn't even on the table." María looked slightly embarrassed as if ashamed that she was so predictable. "I know the rules of the kitchen — no kids in the kitchen till dinner's done. We're gonna go socialize, okay?"

Elena's mother tsked at her, but grabbed her apron off of the cabinet and pulled the spatula out of its pocket to point it at the two of them.

"You will both sit next to me at dinner. I will make sure you eat, and I want to hear all about classes and your exams." Elena looked as if she wanted to protest, but María cut her off. "No excuses, Elena Maria!"

"Ay, Mama!" Elena exclaimed defensively. "We will sit next to you. School is not as interesting as you think it is, though."

María raised her eyebrows at her daughter, and it was clear at that moment where Elena had gotten her spirit and facial expressions from.

"Bueno." María whirled around and began directing Elena's aunts and uncles again, like a conductor cueing instruments in a symphony. Elena shook her head at her mother's back, then gestured for her awestruck friend to follow her out of the room.

~

ELENA DEFTLY WOVE through the crowds of her relatives, leading Cora by the hand again. It seemed the easiest way to not get separated - or at least a good excuse. In all honesty, neither one of them actually wanted to let go of the other, nor did they want to admit to that fact.

They found the platform that Cora had admired on the way in. There was an entire village there, complete with moving ice skaters, scaled down Christmas trees and itty bitty presents. All of it was so intricately designed that it took Cora's breath away. She couldn't even begin to think of how much work had gone into even the planning of a platform like this, let alone building and wiring it.

"This is Mama's favorite part of Christmas," Elena said quietly. "Mine too, honestly."

"I can see why," Cora murmured back. It was a work of art.

Elena glanced over her shoulder, checking to make sure the area behind her was clear. She squatted down and leaned over the village to right one of the skaters that had fallen off of its magnetic track on the rink.

"This guy always falls over. He has ever since I was small. We aren't entirely sure why." Elena dropped down from her squat and crossed her legs under her. She adjusted the skirt of her dress and patted the carpet next to her. "Sit, I'll tell you all about the village."

Cora agreed and knelt down next to the larger woman. She tucked her legs underneath her and adjusted her knee-length skirt around them.

The girls fell into quiet conversation. Elena explained the history of the village, pointing out which houses she loved best and why.

"My favorite is this one." She pointed to a house

nestled directly underneath the tree's branches. It looked as if it was carved out of gingerbread.

"Papi told me that it was actually made out of gingerbread when we first got it. I think I was Sofía's age at the time, and he managed to convince me that it was real." She laughed and reached into the village to pull it out. "If you look carefully, you'll see little teeth marks right here in the back corner."

And she could, glancing at the corner of the ceramic house. The conversations and laughing around them fell into the background while they talked, only to be interrupted by the clanging of a loud bell.

Cora jumped at the sound, muttering a curse. She hadn't been expecting anything of the sort.

"It's dinner time," Elena said, laughing heartily at her friend's surprise. "That's Mama's way of announcing it. Gets your attention, doesn't it?"

"You could've warned me." Cora glared at her playfully and began to pull herself up. As she stood, she caught a glimpse of a small clump of foliage hanging from the ceiling.

Elena pulled herself up using the armchair next to her and fluttered her skirt to get the wrinkles out. When she was finished, she found Cora staring at the ceiling.

"What are we looking at?" she asked in a conspiratorial whisper.

"Is that holly? Or is it -" Cora tilted her head and squinted at the burst of green hanging from the ceiling, red berries scattered throughout. "It's mistletoe, isn't it?"

Elena glanced behind them furtively. Most of the family had disappeared into the large dining room.

"It is, in fact, mistletoe," Elena admitted, her tawny skin turning pink. "Mamá always puts it there."

Cora dropped her chin and squinted at Elena for a moment before her face lit up with a smile.

"So you think you're sneaky, huh? If you wanted to kiss me, all you had to do was ask, Elena."

Elena's face turned even redder, and she muttered something.

"What was that?" Cora stepped closer to the larger woman, her face mere inches from Elena's. She could feel her heart pounding in her chest, and her thoughts were taken over by one continuous scream of joy at the thought of kissing Elena.

"I didn't know if you'd say yes," Elena muttered again. Cora's lips parted slightly, and she leaned even closer.

"How's this for a yes?" Cora asked softly.

Elena blinked and softly touched her lips to Cora's.

It was the perfect movie kiss. Cora wrapped her arms around Elena's silk-wrapped waist and tilted her head just enough to deepen the kiss.

Elena sucked Cora's bottom lip into her mouth, and the world around them disappeared. Neither of them could have told you how long they were there, wrapped around each other.

Until they were interrupted by someone clearing their throat a few feet away. The women leaped apart and looked to where the sound had come from. Their chests were heaving slightly and both women tried to calm their breathing and their bright red faces. Elena's mother stood in the doorway, spatula in hand, with an eyebrow raised above a mischievous smile.

"It's time for dinner, you two."

∽

THE REST of the party had been as much of a whirlwind as the beginning. Cora was pretty sure she'd made semi-interesting conversation at dinner with Elena's mother and family, but she couldn't have told anyone what they'd talked about if someone had threatened her life for it.

Cora wrapped her arms around herself, weaving her fingers through the scratchy mesh of her shrug. Every now and then, she stole glances at Elena, who seemed focused on backing out of the packed driveway. Cora reached over and turned the heat on, hoping to make the car warm up quickly.

Elena caught one of the glances as she looked over her shoulder. All of Elena's relatives had parked at angles they must have practiced that made it just barely possible to get out without hitting one of them, or one of the trees.

"Everything okay?" Elena asked, not taking her eyes off her back windshield. "Other than you being cold, I mean."

Cora hated to be cold, and she wasn't shy about making it known to anyone and everyone who was in her presence while she was cold. Elena had jokingly guessed it was because she was so petite and had no hair to keep all of the hot air in her head.

Cora stuck out her tongue at the larger woman with a smile in her eyes. Elena's mouth quirked up into a smile, though her eyes were still focused on driving.

"So your family is a bit different than I expected," Cora ventured after a few moments. "You really act like you feel comfortable around them? I didn't expect that, with all the wailing about your family visiting."

"They aren't the worst," Elena admitted. "Most of my complaining is about them not planning anything ahead of time. I love most of them dearly, but they're so bad at planning."

"I can see why that would bother you, with you being as organized as you are. It's gotta be a struggle when your whole family is so different from you."

"Yeah, but they were cool about the whole being into women thing so I can deal with them being poor planners," Elena said with a slight laugh. "At least they aren't assholes. Small favors, right?"

"That's always a plus." Cora smiled. The car was finally starting to warm up a little bit as they left the neighborhood, and Cora unfolded her arms slightly. "Sweet beautiful heat."

"You wouldn't be so cold if you'd worn a hat," Elena needled her, reminding her that she'd told her she'd need one before they'd left.

Cora rolled her eyes and didn't dignify the teasing with a response.

"If only you didn't care about messing up what little hair you have…."

"Yeah yeah," Cora said, rolling her eyes again. "Alas, I picked good hair, so I could make a good first impression on your family."

"Between that and freezing to death?"

"Yes. I'd rather freeze to death than have them think I had bad hair," Cora said, recognizing the ridiculousness in her statement. She also totally meant it.

Elena threw her head back and laughed. It was a rolling belly laugh that Cora wanted to last forever. Elena couldn't see it, but Cora's skin was glowing pink as she watched the girl she'd kissed earlier that evening with delight.

Honestly, she was impressed that Elena could laugh

that deeply and still drive in a straight line. If she'd tried, she would have been swerving all over the road.

Once her laughs finally subsided into a wide grin, Cora looked at her sideways.

"I totally meant it."

"This is definitely why I keep you around," Elena said with a giggle. She was almost to the exit that would take Cora back to her apartment, and Cora was almost disappointed the night had to end.

"Tonight was a lot of fun," Cora said softly, her eyes still on Elena. "Your family seems awesome."

Elena flicked her eyes at the smaller girl and looked back at the highway.

"I hope you'll get to see more of them in smaller doses," she answered in a voice almost as soft as Cora's. "Mamá and Papi at least."

"I hope so too."

The girls let the conversation trail off in the last few minutes in the car together. As the road rushed by, Elena kept glancing over at the emerald-clad girl in her passenger seat with what looked like worry in her eyes but didn't say anything for a few minutes.

"Look—" Elena said after a few minutes.

"I think—" Cora said at the same time. They both laughed awkwardly.

"I'll go first," Elena said decidedly, her eyes staying fixed firmly on the road. "We should probably talk about the kiss from earlier, and what it means for us. But I don't think it should be tonight, cause I'm tired, and I think you're burnt out on people."

Cora nodded, and a single curl flopped forward.

"So we'll talk about it tomorrow?" She asked a little bit of anxiety threading through her voice.

"If that's okay?" Elena nodded as if she wasn't entirely sure of herself.

"Well, all right then," Cora said, and within a minute, they were sitting in front of her apartment building. "So I'll text you tomorrow?"

"Yeah," Elena said with a smile. "Text me when you're up in the morning."

Chapter 6

THE NEXT MORNING, Elena found herself pacing and talking to herself in her pristine living room.

"What if she felt pressured to kiss me, 'cause of the mistletoe? What if I screwed everything up? I know she said she liked me too, but what if I ruined everything?"

With every question she asked herself, she felt like one of those youtube videos that sped up every time a certain word was said. Making a disgusted noise, she picked up her phone, intending to call Cora and put some action to her anxiety, but her heart leaped at the sight of a text from Cora.

"Gracias a Dios," she muttered. "If she's texting, she probably doesn't hate me. Entirely. She might only hate me a little."

Ugh. Why did her brain always have to spiral into the unreasonable? Elena rubbed her phone on the leg of her pajama pants and typed a good morning text of her own.

Looking at it before she hit send, she added an exclamation point and a smiling and blushing emoji. She reread the message a few more times for good measure, then nodded at her phone while she hit send. The whoosh sound that accompanied it set the butterflies to fluttering in her stomach.

"I am a damn mess," Elena muttered, shaking her head. "I can't live like this. I need to get dressed and bake something."

Elena flounced around the counter into the kitchen, her satin nightgown swooshing around her.

The cold washed over her as she opened the fridge to see what she had. She popped open the carton of eggs and was happy to see she had half a dozen left. Today would be a good day for a brioche. The egg bread would be a sweet addition to the morning and was complicated enough to keep her mind off of her romance.

Elena closed the fridge and slid her phone back open.

"I'm making brioche, wanna come over?" she typed. She hit send without worrying about an emoji. Cora loved bread, especially fresh bread. Elena knew that would bring her over, as long as she wasn't upset.

Elena's phone dinged. Looking at it, the text read, "Be there in an hour with raspberry preserves. Better make extra!"

"Bring me some eggs, then. It's gonna be a process - brioche dough has to chill for 6 hours."

"Then I'm bringing soda and a book, too."

Elena smiled, and turned back to the kitchen, grabbing her apron as she walked. With a much lighter sigh, she got to work.

~

CORA KNOCKED on the apartment door almost exactly an hour later, just as Elena was putting the bowl of dough into the fridge to rest.

"Come in!" Elena yelled, wiping her doughy hands on her apron. It didn't do much good. Brioche dough was incredibly sticky before it cooled, thanks to all of the eggs in the batter.

Cora flung the door open dramatically. It bounced against the doorstep, and swung back towards her, hitting her squarely on her hip.

"Well, that backfired," she said with a laugh. "At least it didn't hit the eggs. Then we would have had to make omelets!"

Closing the door fully behind her, Cora walked into the kitchen, the grocery store bag swinging on her arm.

"You good over there?" Elena asked skeptically. "Hand me the eggs before you break them, woman. You're scaring me."

Cora stuck her tongue out at Elena but handed her the bag anyway. Elena turned and put the preserves in the fridge, keeping the eggs handy on the counter.

"Can you do me a favor?" Elena asked, showing off her doughy hands. "Can you grab the red mixing bowl out of the cupboard there? My hands are too gooey."

"Yeah, of course," Cora answered. Her fingertips grazed Elena's love handles as she maneuvered past her in the kitchen, making Elena jump. Even after the brief touch had ended, Elena could feel it lingering on her sides.

"Sorry, didn't mean to freak you out," Cora apologized quickly. "It's just tight quarters in here, and you got flour on the side of the counter."

"It's okay," Elena said, chewing her lip. "I just wasn't expecting you to touch me, since..." She trailed off, unsure if she wanted to be as straightforward as she was being. "I don't know. I wasn't expecting it.

"Since I didn't say anything last night, right?" Cora finished for her, looking her in the eye. "I thought that might be a problem. Sometimes when my emotions get involved - when I get really angry or really upset about something or really happy, it's just... It's a lot easier for me to write things down? So when you invited me, I wrote this. So, um, here," she finished, feeling her face flush. She pulled a folded piece of stationery out of her back jeans pocket and set it on the counter between them

"I'll, um, let you read that in private. I left my purse in the car." Cora all but sprinted out of the apartment. Elena watched her go, a little bit stunned. Her purse was on the counter right next to the carton of eggs.

"I guess I'll read this then." Elena's still doughy hands stuck lightly to the stationery, which made unfolding the note more difficult than it should have been.

Once it was finally unfolded, Elena saw that it was only a few sentences in Cora's beautiful cursive.

"I think you are absolutely wonderful, and I would love to pursue a relationship with you if that's what you want. I'm ace and sex is kind of a big deal for a lot of people. I hope it isn't a big deal for you. If not, I can make myself content with being your friend.
XO
Cora"

Elena realized the note was the grown-up version of a "do you like me" note from elementary school and couldn't resist a giggle. She set the note on the counter, and wiped her hands on her apron as she went for the door - Cora couldn't have gone far.

Opening the door, she found Cora leaning against the railing of the walkway, studiously staring at her phone. The angle she held her phone at showed that she was just staring at the home screen of her phone, pretending to be busy.

"C'mere, you goose," Elena said with a smile. "Stop playing busy and get back in here."

Cora blushed at getting caught, but followed Elena back into the apartment, closing the door behind her.

"So, you read it?" She asked, chewing lightly on the inside of her mouth.

"I read it," Elena confirmed, desperately wanting to hold Cora. "You know I don't care that you don't want sex, right? That's so not a deal breaker for me. Especially if the deal is you being a part of my life."

"I just…" Cora trailed off, shifting her weight from foot to foot. Her eyes welled up. "It's been an issue before, and you're way too important as a part of my life for it to be an issue."

"It isn't an issue for me," Elena assured the small woman. "Sex is just sex. Time spent with you is a gift."

The tears that had been welling up in Cora's eyes began to spill over.

"Can I hug you right now?" she asked, looking like she desperately needed it.

Elena took off her apron and wrapped her up in a hug without hesitation.

Cora's chin fell right in Elena's cleavage, but neither of them seemed to care at that moment.

"Well this moved quickly, didn't it?" Elena joked softly.

"Want me to move?" Cora asked, her voice thick with emotion.

"Hush," Elena said soothingly. She held her, rubbing circles into Cora's back as she cried. "I've got you."

"I don't want you to go," Cora mumbled into her chest. "I don't want to lose you."

"I've got you," she repeated. "I'm not going anywhere unless you want me to."

They stood like that for nearly ten minutes, just holding each other. Cora's tears subsided, and she pulled an arm away from where it had been wrapped around Elena's waist to wipe her eyes.

"Well, that was embarrassing," she laughed wetly. "Probably should have included that I cry a lot in the note."

Elena smiled down at her, her tongue poking out between her teeth.

"Your note was adorable, just like you, you goose." Cora smiled up at her crookedly through still wet eyelashes. "And I already knew you cry a lot. I've seen you read. I like you, Cora. We'll figure out the rest together. Sound good?"

Elena looked down at her expectantly. Cora bit her lip and continued to smile up at her girlfriend. The thought of the word "girlfriends" being applied to them made Elena's heart sing.

"Sounds good to me."

Elena pressed a kiss to Cora's forehead.

"Now, do you want to learn how to make brioche?

"Sure," Cora said with a grin. "That sounds fun."

The Final Interview

The Final Interview was originally distributed as an exclusive short story for my newsletter. It takes place before the events of Wrapped Up In You! Enjoy!

The Final Interview: A Short Story

ELENA STOOD by the door tapping her fingers anxiously against the leather exterior of her purse. It was almost time for her to leave for the hopefully final interview for a new job at a local law firm. She really wanted this job, and her anxiety had kicked into high gear.

"Are you sure you've got everything you need?" Cora asked, still in the shorts and t-shirt that she'd slept in.

Elena had gone through her bag at least half a dozen times that morning.

She was positive that she wasn't forgetting anything, but the little voice in the back of her head was telling her otherwise.

The little voice was often a liar, but she felt like she really was forgetting something today.

"I'm pretty sure...." Elena grimaced. "Can you check behind me?"

"Sure thing, love. Hand over your bag."

Elena handed over the purse, and Cora promptly sat

on the floor. She crossed her legs like they taught you to in kindergarten. She went through it, ticking things off on her fingers as she went. "You really need to clean out your purse. You have so much change at the bottom of this!"

"Now is really not the time, Cora... Just help me make sure I haven't forgotten anything for this interview, would you?"

Cora flapped a hand at her.

"Of course, of course. I know what you forgot!"

Elena raised her eyebrows, but Cora just got up and walked into her office. She came back out, but Elena couldn't figure out what she'd retrieved from it.

"Close your eyes and hold out your hand!" Cora said in a sing-song voice, a silly grin on her face.

She did so, but not without making a face at her girlfriend. Something small and cold dropped into her hand, and she opened her eyes. Her keys. She'd forgotten her keys.

"You are the best, Cora."

"I'm not done yet! You forgot one more thing."

"Oh? What's that?"

Cora smiled impishly up at Elena.

"A kiss for good luck!"

"Well, I can fix that."

Elena set down her purse and keys just in time for Cora to rise up on the tips of her toes to press a deep, luxurious kiss to Elena's lips. She didn't hesitate to return the kiss, wrapping the much smaller girl in her arms.

By the time they separated, they were both more than a little breathless.

"Now... have I forgotten anything else?"

"Nope," Cora said, popping the last consonant in the

word emphatically. "You're all set. Go kick their butts and bring home all the money, babe!"

THE END

Cover Artist: Ceillie Simkiss

It's been two years since Cora and Elena of LEARNING CURVES discovered how easy it is to learn to love—but

with Christmas just around the bend, they're going to
have to learn to cope when both their families descend
on their household for the first time ever. With her
brothers and parents underfoot and a million dishes to
cook, it's hard enough for Elena to plan her double
surprise for Elena, even harder when she has to corral
her wayward brothers into it—but when Cora's own
surprise plans tangle with Elena's, it may be impossible
to tie up the holiday in a neat little bow.

There's mayhem and laughter, warmth and unexpected
turns—and even if it all doesn't go according to plan,
neither Cora nor Elena care so long as they can stay
wrapped up in each other.

Chapter 1

CORA'S EYES SHOT OPEN. Her heart raced inside her chest, and she had no idea why. The room around her was still the deep dark of the wee hours of the morning and she could feel the warmth and weight of Elena's body in the bed next to her. She eased herself up in bed, leaning against the headboard. She rubbed her eyes gently with the tips of her index fingers. Slowly, she realized what had woken her. From her spot in bed, she could hear a chorus of voices… and it sounded like they were singing.

Cora grabbed her phone from the nightstand and saw that it was just barely 5 a.m. She stifled a groan as she eased herself out of the bed so that she wouldn't wake Elena. She was not a morning person at the best of times.

Did I leave music playing in the office? She asked herself, but knew as soon as the thought crossed her mind that that wasn't what she was hearing.

Wrapping herself in her warmest flannel robe, she

shuffled her way towards the front door, trying to discover the source of the sound.

She thought she could hear a few children's voices in the group, which was the most confusing part. She and Elena had moved out to the outskirts of our small town in Virginia specifically so that their neighbors wouldn't make weird noises in the middle of the night. Their nearest neighbors only had one daughter, and there was no way that she would be out this early in the morning. Janelle was famous in her family for her ability to sleep in, no matter what the occasion.

The closer she got to the front door, the more confused she got. She knew the tunes of the songs that the group was singing, but didn't recognize any of the words. When the chorus transitioned into the Little Drummer Boy, she realized why. The group was singing in Spanish.

Tugging the flannel robe tighter around herself, she tied the belt as close as she could around her slim waist to keep herself to keep the heat in. She pulled her shoulder-length blonde curls out from underneath the collar and ran her finger through them.

She had no idea what her hair looked like, but since whoever was out there was showing up unexpectedly at 5 AM on Christmas Eve, she didn't particularly care.

Something clicked inside Cora's mind. She suddenly knew exactly what she would find when she opened the front door. A gust of cold air seeped through the door as she opened it to reveal a frost-patterned storm door. Through it, Cora could see the outline of Elena's parents, her three brothers, and Anton's two children, Sofia and David.

With a sigh that became visible in the cold air, she

slid her feet into her faux fur lined house slippers and stepped out onto the porch.

"Señora Mendéz, what is this? I thought you weren't coming until this afternoon."

They stopped singing and trudged up the porch steps.

"This is an asaltó navideño, Cora!" Elena's eldest brother Anton answered in a chipper voice that was completely inappropriate for the time of day. "This is a Mendéz family tradition with new members. Now let us in before the kids freeze to death!"

Sofía made a show out of rolling her eyes and chattering her teeth as only a nine-year-old could. Cora beckoned them all into the house, closing the door tightly behind me with a shiver. When they got to the kitchen, Cora was the only one surprised to find Elena at the stove pouring water into the electric kettle.

Elena turned towards her girlfriend, her loosely braided hair swinging with the movement of her curvy body and a wide grin spreading across her face. Cora was beginning to feel played.

"You, madam, are a fiend!" Cora squealed. "You knew this was coming?"

Elena nodded, her smile becoming wickeder.

"You could have warned me!"

"Now where's the fun in that?" Elena's laugh boomed through the kitchen and was joined by chuckles from her brothers. Cora glared. "You had a nice Christmas surprise, no? I got to watch you stumble to the door in a confused, sleep-drunk stupor. That alone made it worth it to me."

As she flipped the switch on the kettle, Elena flashed her a wide, dazzling smile that would almost be enough to make Cora forgive her. Almost.

Her voice came out in a whine.

"Elena, it's 5:15 in the morning. I've never been up this early of my own volition."

"And you still aren't. You're gonna be just fine, you big baby." She pressed a kiss to Cora's forehead and pushed her gently towards the back of the house. "Go take a shower. I'll take care of getting the hungry masses their breakfast."

Cora walked away shaking her head. Behind her, she heard Elena give her first order of the day. She could see the image in her head. Elena would be standing with one hand on her wide hips and the other would be brandishing a spatula like a scepter. She knew it well.

"I'm making scrambled eggs and baking bacon. If anyone has any complaints, keep them to yourself because I don't care. You invade my house, you deal with my cooking, claro?"

Her family's chatter filled the warm air of their home as Cora made her way to the back of the house to get ready for what was shaping up to be a very long Christmas Eve day.

THERE WAS VERY little that Elena loved more than the sound of her family chattering amongst themselves. It was great to have them here in their dining room together for the first time.

The chairs didn't match the table or each other, and they didn't have any placemats, but she didn't care. They didn't seem to care either. It felt like Mama had wrapped a cozy weighted blanket around Elena and tucked her in to read a bedtime story like she had when Elena was little.

She served the last bit of scrambled eggs to Sofía and David just in time for Cora to re-enter the kitchen. She still looked tired, but she seemed a little more human than she had before she'd showered.

She wore loose black-and-white striped pants and the hems rustled against the hardwood floor as she made her way to the stove. Elena couldn't get over how wonderful it was to watch Cora walk around in the house that they were renting together. Every time she walked in the door to see Cora working at the dining room table, or laying out an art project on the living room floor, she couldn't help falling in love with her all over again.

Cora pressed a kiss to Elena's cheek, carefully avoiding leaning over the still hot pans. Sparks of a different sort spread across Elena's face at the comforting press of Cora's lips. Even though they'd been dating for more than two years at this point. Elena hoped that they never lost that spark.

The toaster popped, releasing two slices of homemade rye bread and surprising them both.

Cora pulled back and smiled. Elena felt a matching goofy grin spread across her own face.

"Are you hungry, honey? Pan's still hot."

Cora wrinkled her freckled nose and grumbled.

"It's way too early for real food," she grumbled. "I will, however, have some toast."

She grabbed a piece from the toaster and yelped, nearly dropping it from the heat.

Mama laughed quietly at her but didn't say anything. Elena rolled her eyes and fussed at her girlfriend.

"At least grab a plate, would you? We got those cute ones for a reason!"

Mama laughed out loud at the admonition that Cora

ignored. She chose, instead, to slather her toast in butter in her hand. Elena rolled her eyes.

After taking a few bites, Cora glanced around the room and then back to Elena.

"Elena, have you eaten anything?"

Elena looked down at the stove in front of her and realized that she hadn't.

"I've had a cup of coffee?"

"Elena Maria!" Mama chided her. "That is not breakfast!"

"I was cooking for y'all! When was I supposed to eat?" she defended herself

"No excuse!" Cora told her, wagging a crumb-covered finger at her. "Sit and finish your coffee. I'll make you breakfast."

Elena glanced at the smaller girl dubiously. Her cooking skills had improved since they had graduated from grad school, but only marginally.

"You sure you're up for that? It's awfully early for you to be cooking in front of people."

Cora stuck her tongue out at Elena.

"Would I have offered if I wasn't up for it? No. Now go sit down with your family."

Elena obeyed, handing over her spatula ceremoniously. She grabbed her half-drunk mug of coffee and made her way over to one of the two empty seats at the table.

As she let the noise of her family wash over her, she was glad that they had prepared to have a separate kids table for dinner. If they hadn't, there was no way that there would be enough space for Cora's family to join them.

"You want your eggs sunny side up, right, hon?"

Elena nodded with a smile, watching as Cora

cracked two eggs into the still warm hand with a practiced hand. She seasoned them lightly and put down a few slices of rye toast for Elena as well. If Elena hadn't known better, she would've thought that Cora really did know what she was doing in the kitchen.

Sofía had managed to maneuver herself so that she was directly next to Elena at the table after finishing her breakfast. She pressed her slightly sticky face to Elena's shoulder affectionately.

"Tía Elena, I love your Christmas tree! It's so preeeeeeetty! And there's so much tree in it!"

Her father tried to hide a laugh behind a bite of toast. Elena didn't bother. She laughed loudly, pressing a kiss to Sofía's tiny brown forehead. The tree that Cora and Elena had picked out was just barely 5 feet tall and had significantly fewer ornaments then Sofía would be used to seeing on a Christmas tree.

As soon as Elena drew her lips away from Sofía's forehead, wrinkled in confusion.

"Qué? Why is that funny?"

"It's funny because you're cute, Fi," Marianne told her with a pleased smile.

"That doesn't make any sense, Mama, but whatever. Tía's tree is so pink and yellow! How come her tree doesn't have all the colors that Abuela's does?"

"Abuela has collected all of her ornaments over a very long time," Elena told her. "This is the first year that Cora and I have a Christmas tree, so we didn't have that many ornaments. We decided to go with our favorite colors for our Christmas tree this year."

"But Tía Elena, you don't like pink that much!"

"No, but I do," Cora butted in. "Pink is my favorite."

She had snuck up behind the family while they talked. Cora reached a sweatshirt-clad arm around

Elena's broad shoulders to place a beautiful plate of food in front of her on the table. The runny egg yolks spilled out ever so slightly towards the perfectly toasted bread. Elena had to admit that she was impressed.

She scooped up a bit of egg and placed it onto the toast before taking a bite. She found that it was cooked and seasoned exactly the way she liked it.

"This is delicious, Cor! Thank you for making it for me."

She nudged Elena's shoulder and teased her gently.

"You don't have to sound so surprised, El."

Elena smiled crookedly up at her and Cora pressed a kiss to her forehead. Luís and Gabriel awwed pretentiously, trying to ruin the moment.

Elena stuck her tongue out at them, making the rest of the table laugh.

"Well, boys, since you have enough time to be jerks to your sister, you can do the dishes," Papí announced.

Their awws turned to groans as if they were surprised by this turn of events. It was Cora's turn to laugh. "It's only fair and you know it."

The kids were mostly blinking heavily at their plates. Now that they were in the warmth of the house and their stomachs were full, they were wiped.

"Everything in the sink, kids," Cora instructed them. "Elena, take your time eating. How about we all go take a nap in the living room, eh?"

The children happily followed her instructions, following her to the sink and then out of the room like ducklings after their mother. It was adorable. Mamá followed after them as if she was ready for a nap herself.

Papí smiled over at Elena, his thick eyebrows raised slightly.

"You didn't think we'd miss out on the chance to surprise you here, did you?"

She laughed, covering her mouth to hide the half-chewed food in it. She swallowed it and answered him.

"I kind of expected this. Do you remember the time we drove three hours in the middle of the night to sing at Anton's place when he and Marianne first moved in together?"

Papí's chest rumbled with a laugh of his own, one that Luís echoed.

Anton had moved in with a few girlfriends over the years, but the whole family had known that Marianne was the best match for him. That Christmas had been particularly memorable because Marianne had come running out of the house with her hair in curlers. She groaned at the memory.

"Or the time Luís moved in with that accountant?" Gabriel piped up. "I thought that guy was gonna call the police on us! At least I fed you."

"What did you expect my *platonic* white roommate to do when you show up at 4 o'clock in the morning singing Spanish Christmas carols?" Luís protested. "this tradition is supposed to be for romantic partners, not moving in with a roommate from work."

"Yeah, well, since you're aromantic, we had to work with what we could get," Anton retorted. "You don't miss out on family traditions just because romance isn't something you're interested in."

Luís shrugged like he didn't care, but there was a glint of something that looked like gratitude in his eyes before he looked back down at the plates he was clearing.

"Fair enough. Plus, it helped me figure out whether or not he was a good roommate."

"Newsflash!" Gabriel chimed in. "He wasn't. He was the worst about doing any housework."

The whole table laughed at that. It was true. The guy was known for leaving his laundry in the washer or dryer for days on end. His mother had clearly done his laundry until he moved out on his own, something Mama had never tolerated from any of her children.

"He only lasted on his own for like six months, right?"

"Yeah, I'm pretty sure he moved back in with his mom." Luís rolled his eyes.

Elena washed down the remainder of her breakfast with her coffee as the table laughed. She was fully awake now and was excited for the day full of sneaking and family ahead of her.

Her brothers were clearing the table still, so she leaned forward and shoved her plate toward them.

"Y'all ready to help me make this the happiest Christmas that Cora's ever had?"

They grinned back at her, knowing exactly the plan that she had in store. All three answered her at the same time.

"Absolutamente, Elena."

MARÍA AND CORA laid out pallets made of blankets and couch cushions for Sofia and David. They were asleep in minutes and she wistfully thought how nice it would be to join them for a nap. She shook the thought away with a sigh. A nap was not in her future today.

Elena had told her about this tradition, but Cora had been so preoccupied with both of their families to visit for Christmas that the thought that this might happen hadn't even occurred to her.

Cora wouldn't have traded being a part of the family tradition for anything. She wouldn't have minded it if they came two or three hours later, though, for the sake of a good night's sleep.

They still had a lot of cleaning and food prep to do to be ready for Christmas Eve dinner. The Mendéz family had brought more food than she thought they would ever be able to eat. Cora was in charge of the ham and Elena was in charge of the shrimp scampi. Everything else had been farmed out to their various family members.

Luís was making kid-friendly coquito, and Cora's mother was bringing Cora's favorite apple pie when she arrived later in the evening. Maríahad decided that she was going to surprise the family with the sides that they were making.

Cora had been testing glaze recipes on Elena for weeks, trying to find the perfect one. They had decided on a mixture of spices, minced garlic and red wine vinegar. It had been marinating on the 10-pound spiral ham for several days. Cora found herself praying that it turned out well at the end of the night.

She desperately didn't want to disappoint the Mendézes or her own parents. Neither she nor Elena had anything to prove to their families, but it was the first time that they were hosting them both in their new home.

For once, Elena was not as anxious about it as Cora was. Perhaps because it was small compared to her usual family Christmases, but larger than the ones that Cora was used to. Both women also had tasks of their own to take care of on this busy Christmas Eve.

Elena had to finish the grocery shopping with her brothers.

Cora's two tasks were to pick up the homemade paper Christmas crackers that were part of her family tradition, and the ring that she had chosen to propose to Elena with as soon as their families had left for the night.

They were not particularly hard tasks, but she was anxious nonetheless. She figured she might as well get it out of the way, which meant getting dressed properly. Cora made her way back to the bedroom, grabbing her thickest forest green knitted sweater and sliding it over the black T-shirt she'd worn to breakfast.

It, combined with the thick wool socks she wouldn't go without, would do well to keep her warm despite the below freezing temperatures outside. It was one of the coldest winters she could remember and she hated to have to go out in it. She might even have to wear a hat, she thought with a shudder.

María poked her head into the bedroom.

"You said that you had some errands to run. Would you like some company?"

Cora smiled happily.

"I would love some company! It shouldn't take too long to do the errands I had planned. Was there anything you needed to do?"

"Oh, no. Elena is going to pick up the last of the things that we need from the store, and she's gonna take the boys with her. Manuel and Maríanne are going to stay here with children, so I thought I would offer my assistance to you instead of sitting here waiting for it to be time to cook."

"That sounds great. Let me grab my coat and wallet and I can give you the penny tour around town while we're out."

María beamed back at the younger woman, and Cora nearly blushed from the intensity of her motherly affection. Even two years later, she still wasn't used to the amount of affection that María was capable of sharing.

She left the room and Cora heard her telling her husband and daughter-in-law of her new plans for the morning. Cora grabbed her black hooded coat from the closet and walked to the door where she'd left her boots. María was already there, bundling herself up in a double-breasted red peacoat and black knit cap.

She slid her feet into the black ankle boots and poked her head into the kitchen. Elena's brothers were still working on the dishes and talking amongst themselves while Elena supervised.

"Hey, hon, I'm headed out with your mother. We should be back in about an hour?"

Elena nodded and blew a kiss across the kitchen.

"I'm taking these hooligans with me, so we won't be here when you get back. Have fun and be safe, love."

Cora smiled softly and returned the blown kiss.

"Right back at you, El."

ONCE THE DOOR shut behind Cora and María, Elena couldn't keep the smile off of her face. The excitement that she had been working to hide from her girlfriend bubbled out of her in a pleased giggle.

She wasn't known for being able to keep secrets well for this exact reason. If Cora had not been as anxious about getting their new house ready for Christmas, Elena didn't know how she would have been able to keep it from her.

She had been planning this particular evening for

months. Cora had always dreamed of a Christmas proposal and Elena intended to give it to her with some adjustments of her own. Everything was ready, except that she didn't have either her Christmas present or the ring in hand yet.

With some strategic teamwork, Elena and her brothers would be picking up the groceries her family had forgotten, the specially designed engagement ring from the jeweler, *and* picking up the small white West Highland terrier that Cora had fallen in love with from the animal shelter. It would be a busy day.

Elena and her brothers had always had a strong relationship ranging from best friends to worst enemies, but now that they were grown, that relationship was best described as partners in crime.

There would be no crimes committed by them today, but they were being sneaky. Between the three of them, it would be a light afternoon's work. Elena was sure that everything would get done in time thanks to her planning.

She had hoped that she would be able to send one of her brothers to the grocery store on his own, but they had all ridden up together in Anton's minivan, which they needed to leave with Marianne in case they needed to go somewhere with the kids. That meant that they would need to pile into Elena's burnt orange SUV and work strategically to get everything done in time to be back and hide the dog before Cora returned with María and the Christmas crackers.

Elena walked into the living to watch her oldest brother press soft kisses onto the foreheads of his sleeping children and his smiling wife's lips. She left them to bundle up against the cold weather outdoors.

Once they had said their goodbyes, Anton, Gabriel,

and Luís piled into Elena's SUV with minimal fighting about who got to ride shotgun. If there had been anyone else needing to get in, they wouldn't have fit. Anton and Gabriel were both tall and fat like Elena was. Luís was tall, too, but he was built more like a beanpole then a stockpot like the other three siblings.

She turned the car on to start warming up the air around them. Elena's hands were slightly shaky from the excitement, so she clasped them together to tell her brothers the plan for the day.

"Okay, boys, here's the plan," she started, as if she was telling them the play on a football field. "We pick up the dog from the foster parent's house. We take her to the groomers. Luís, we're going to leave you there to be there while she's groomed and make sure she's done well, okay?"

He nodded and she continued.

"From there, I'm dropping Gabriel at the grocery store to pick up some last minute things. I've got the list of everything Máma needs to make the side dishes she wants."

"Wait, what's my job?" Anton interrupted.

"You, my good sir, are coming with me to go get the ring. You've done this before, so I wanted to keep you with me. Once we have the ring, I'll swing back to get Gabriel and then Luís. Everybody good with that?"

She looked each of them in the eye and they nodded their assent.

"All right, let's roll!"

∽

Chapter 2

THE INTERIOR of Cora's beat up green Subaru was frigid. She started the engine and flipped the heat on, blasting it towards the windshield to defrost it without blowing the inevitably cold air at her future mother-in-law in the passenger seat.

We waited in companionable silence for several minutes while the windshield heated from the interior. She rubbed her hands over her undercut trying to warm it. In the back of her head, Elena's lightly accented voice was scolding her for not wearing a hat.

As usual, that voice was absolutely correct, and Cora knew she should have been wearing something on her head, but she couldn't stand the thought of having to worry about having a bad hair day today of all days.

As the car warmed around them, Cora turned on the radio. All of the stations were playing Christmas carols at this time of year and María began to hum along quietly to Carol of the Bells

When the windshield was clear, Cora turned the knob so that the now-warm air was blowing on them both. It made it comfortable enough for her to drive within a few minutes.

"Thank you for including us in your family tradition, María. It means so much to me, and I know it means even more to Elena."

Her smile became a confused one, her eyebrows wrinkling like something Cora had said wasn't making sense.

"Of course you are part of our traditions. You know full well that no one even tangentially related to our family gets left out of things like this."

The wipers cleared the last of the frost's beautiful crystals from the windshield. It felt as if it cleared the confusion from María's thoughts as well.

"You thought it would be because you are gay? Mi hija, you know that is not how our family works."

Cora tensed her hands on the steering wheel, trying to warm it enough so that she could leave her hands on it comfortably and drive.

"I know, but, well… I try not to get my hopes up when it comes to family traditions."

María nodded sagely but laid a loving hand on the sleeve of Cora's coat.

"You are our family, darling, and we will never leave you out unless you want to be left out."

Cora felt a lump form in her throat that had nothing to do with the cold. She tried to swallow it and blinked back tears at the same time. Failing that, she started to back out of their steep driveway.

For several minutes, the only sound in the car was the quiet tinkling of Christmas-themed commercials.

"So, you want to propose to Elena, eh?" María said after a few moments.

Cora spluttered, nearly veering off the road.

"What? How did you know that?"

"Well, I peeked in your office. You'd left a note next to your laptop to pick up the ring. But also, there's nothing else you need for this holiday, and you and Elena are brilliantly happy together. What else could you need to pick up today other than a ring?"

Cora threw her head back and laughed. Of course, in the hour she'd been in the house, she'd made her way into the office.

"You are a force of nature, Señora Mendéz. I should know better than to underestimate you."

"You should know better than to call me Señora Mendéz by now, Cora dear. It's María, as I've told you time and time again. Especially now that you're going to be family for real."

"You think she'll say yes?" Cora asked nervously. She was almost positive that she would. They'd had several conversations about marriage as a nebulous future thing, but they'd never put a date on it.

María scoffed at the question. Even though Cora kept her eyes on the road, she knew that she would be rolling her eyes in the exact picture of her daughter. She couldn't help but grin shyly.

"Of course she will say yes. When you know someone is right for you, you know. And Elena knew a long time ago."

Cora knew that she was at risk of bursting into full on sobs while driving. The last few days had been emotional ones, and today had been guaranteed to be the same. A few tears leaked down her face, to her dismay.

"Look what you did," Cora said with a wet laugh, using one hand to wipe them away. She kept the other hand firmly on the wheel. It would turn into the worst

Christmas possible if she wrecked her car with her future mother-in-law in the car.

"Pssh. You cry at the drop of a hat. Es adorable, mi hija. But you must focus on the road. I do not know how to get to the store we are going to, or I would offer to drive."

That made Cora laugh harder, and shook the rest of the moisture from her face. Elena had clearly learned her conversational skills from her mother.

"What articles are you working on right now? She asked pointedly. "Anything fun?"

Cora shrugged her shoulders.

"Holidays tend to slow everything down, so I'm not working on a lot right now. I did just finish a book for review that I thought you might like."

She perked up. María loved to read, particularly romance and mystery novels, and so far Cora had a perfect batting average when it came to recommendations.

"Well, this one is part of a serial detective story, like a TV show. It's super slow on the romance aspect, and it's great."

Cora gave her a general summary of *Criminal Intentions*, leading to a discussion of other stories they'd read recently. By the time they arrived at the jeweler's, Cora was calm and cheerful. Even the butterflies in her stomach had settled for the first time since she'd woken up.

María bustled around the car and opened the door for Cora before she could even unbuckle her seatbelt.

"Here's to the next step of your life, and becoming family."

Without another word, the two women swept into the store.

∼

GRAVEL CRUNCHED under the SUV's tires as Elena pulled up to the home where her dog had been living for the last three weeks. Elena was both excited and nervous as she put the car in park in front of the sprawling yellow ranch style house.

Elena knew that the foster parent had several cats, which was why she was sending Luis in to fetch their new family member. She wished she could go in herself, but couldn't risk an allergy attack that she knew would happen if she went into the house. There was no way that a proposal could be romantic when the proposer's eyes were swollen shut because of smelling a cat. Plus, it would upset the dog, not to mention her brothers, to have to spend several hours in the ER with her after she used her EpiPen.

"Okay, Luis, you're with me. I can't go into the house so I'll need y'all's help carrying her crate and things out to the car. I'm just going to the door with you so that Ms. Libby doesn't think you're here to steal her dog or something. I'm not sure she's ever seen a Puerto Rican in person before."

Anton snorted. All three of her brothers slid out of the car. Once they were onto the gravel of the driveway, each of them began to stretch like they'd been in the car for hours instead of the 20 minutes it took to get across town. Elena rolled her eyes at them and started walking towards the house, knowing they would follow her.

The closer she got, the louder the cacophony of yelling animals became. She could hear dogs barking, alerting to her approach, and cats meowing through the walls of the woman's house. She was almost willing to risk the allergy attack to see just how many animals she actually had in her home. Almost.

Elena's brothers caught up to her when she reached the extremely Christmassy porch. Multi-colored twinkle lights hung from every possible post, and a few slightly weathered snowflake decorations hung between them. Elena thought it was pretty, in an excessive way.

She rang the doorbell and the barking began anew.

"Want to take bets that Elena's dog is the yappiest?" Gabriel asked. Even without turning, she knew that he was smirking at her.

"I'm absolutely certain my dog will not be the yappiest in there," Elena insisted, just in time for the screen door to open in her face.

She took a step back to avoid getting hit by the smallest old woman she thought she'd ever met. The old woman had a messy bun of gray hair on top of her head and apparently a negative amount of body fat. Elena was pretty sure that she could count every bone in her body, despite the bright pink, puffy coat she wore.

Two orange tabby kittens shot past everyone standing on the porch and directly up the large magnolia tree. The woman rubbed her forehead with a groan.

"You must be Ms. Mendéz. And who are these lovely gentlemen?"

She ran her hazel eyes over the Mendéz brothers appreciatively. Elena smiled.

"These are my brothers, Ms. Libby. They came to help me get the dog you've been fostering for me, since I'm allergic to cats. Speaking of, are you worried about those two?"

Libby waved a hand at the tree, where the cats were lounging behind the large leaves, batting playfully at each other.

"Sage and Paprika are the naughtiest of my foster kittens. They'll come back when they're cold and yell to be let in."

"If you say so..." Elena trailed off dubiously. It was far too cold out there for humans, let alone for cats that were much bigger than her size 12 shoe, but she certainly wasn't going to go after them.

"It'll be all right, dear. Now, come on in, you strapping young men. You're liable to get jumped on by one of my dogs, but if you say 'Down' they oughta listen. They just get awful excited..." Her voice trailed off as she turned the corner in the house. The boys followed her as best as they could, navigating around the countless animals at their feet.

Through the screen door, Elena could see a beautiful brown standard poodle, a large, goofy-looking German Shepherd, some sort of Chihuahua mix and three calico cats wandering around her brothers' feet. She could hear other dogs barking from further inside the house, and was grateful that she wasn't going in. With as much noise as she could hear outside, she could only imagine how badly the sounds on the interior would set off her anxiety on top of the allergies.

She walked back to the car, admiring the beautiful rows of trees in the huge yard around her. She could imagine that it would be absolutely stunning during fall when the leaves were changing. She popped open the back hatch of her SUV and grimaced at the amount of loose paper in it.

"I can't put her in her crate back here with it looking like this," Elena scolded herself. "Time to tidy all of this up."

Without any further ado, she pulled her briefcase to

the front of the trunk and began cleaning to prepare for her new family member.

FIFTEEN MINUTES LATER, Elena and her brothers had learned that the dog did not particularly like being in the crate in the trunk. Her whining was nearly deafening, even to Elena's ears at the front of the car. The dog had been thoroughly groomed.

In a stroke of genius, Luis had picked up a beautiful length of tartan ribbon from the craft store he had wandered through while he had waited for the dog to be groomed.

"Gabriel, this dog sounds like you when you were little," Anton joked. "Always with the whining."

"Yeah, yeah," Gabriel replied. "At least I was cute."

"Hey! My dog is cute, too!" Elena objected. The dog punctuated her objection with a loud yip. The humans burst into laughter.

"She seems fine enough when we're on the highway," Luis noted.

Elena could see in the rearview mirror that he was turned nearly all the way around in his seat to pet the dog in her crate. It seemed to help her calm down and stop whining, so Elena didn't say anything. They were nearly home. Which meant, it was time to deviate from the path her brothers expected to take.

"Elena, is this the way to your house? I don't remember these houses."

"We are going home, sort of. We can't take this lady home yet. I want her to be a surprise this evening. Luckily, our neighbor has four acres of land and more dogs than we can keep track of."

At that, she caught a glimpse of Luis whipping around in his seat.

"Wait, you're surprising your girlfriend with a dog for Christmas? Elena, you know better than to give surprise animals!"

She rolled her eyes. He was right - she did know better than to give surprise animals. But this was different.

"Cora went and saw this dog at the shelter three times in two weeks. I know she wants her. She even picked out a name for her before the shelter told her that she'd been adopted by someone else."

That someone else, of course, had been Elena. As soon as the dog realized Luis's hands weren't on her, she started whining again.

"You are sneaky, sister. I approve, even if the dog is whiny as hell. What's the name?"

"You'll find out tonight. I won't spoil the surprise, even for you three."

She drove up a long gravel driveway that wound through fenced in pastures. It was the back entrance to their neighbor's property, and the only way that Elena was sure to get the dog into Adelaide's house without being spotted by Cora's eagle eyes. The house they pulled up at was much grander than theirs. It was a proper pillared southern farmhouse with white siding and bright blue shutters that Elena always found striking.

"These people make bank, don't they?" Anton asked with a surprised laugh.

"They really do," she admitted. "I think the house is actually inherited from his side of the family, but he does something that makes him a ton of money. I don't know him that well yet, but I love his wife and daughter. Your kids know them, Anton. Janelle is Sofía's age."

He rubbed the back of his head thoughtfully.

"Wait, Janelle is real? I thought that was just her imaginary friend. Whoops."

Gabriel and Luis burst into laughter in the backseat, which set the dog to barking again.

Elena sighed, a little exasperated and frazzled, as she parked the car next to the screened-in wrap around porch.

"Y'all are a damn mess, you know that? Now get out and help me get her inside without causing a panic, please."

"Aye, aye, captain." Gabriel punctuated the remark with a mocking salute.

~

CORA AND MARÍA beat Elena and the boys home, which wasn't surprising. They had only been gone for maybe 45 minutes. She couldn't imagine how busy the only grocery store in town would be on Christmas Eve. Besides, it gave her time to hide the ring and help get everything set up for dinner.

As soon as they got out of the car, high-pitched voices assailed them from the field next door.

"Tía Cora! Abuela! C'mere!"

"Miss Cora!"

She knew those sounds. Janelle and Sofía had found each other already, and David was toddling along after them. A glance confirmed it, and that the three were surrounded by dogs, as usual. Marianne watched from the neighbor's porch.

"Quien es?"

"Hey Janelle!" she yelled across the yard. Their nine-year-old neighbor waved back furiously. "That's our neighbor Janelle. She and Sofía have become very good friends in the times that she's visited us."

"They have so many dogs! Where do they put them?"

"I'm pretty sure they foster some for the local animal shelter," Cora laughed. "Plus they have 3 acres and a heated barn."

"Oh, I see. And they are nice people? The dogs will not bite Sofía or David?"

María still looked slightly concerned, so Cora laid a gloved hand on her shoulder comfortingly. María looked down at her skeptically.

"The dogs are safe and the people are lovely. It looks like Adelaide is coming out now. Would you like to go and meet her?"

She thought for a moment and then nodded firmly. The grass, still slightly frosted over, crunched underneath their feet as they made their way across the side yards. The five dogs of varying sizes raced towards them, leaping up on Cora and sniffing at María's feet and legs.

"Everybody, down," Cora told them with as much authority as she could muster before laughing and scratching each of their ears in turn. She heard Adelaide's loud braying laugh behind them, and looked up to see the short, stout woman standing there with a mug of something steaming in her hands.

"Merry Christmas, Cora! How did the asaltó navideño go this morning?" Her country accent butchered the Spanish words, even though she was trying.

María laughed loudly at the cheesy grin on Adelaide's dark brown, freckled face, and the frown that had formed on Cora's.

"Am I the only one who didn't know about that?"

"Well, Elena didn't want one of us to hear singing at the crack of dawn and call the police, so probably," she drawled. She turned to María and stretched out her gloved hand.

"I'm Adelaide, the neighbor. You must be Mrs. Mendéz. It's a pleasure to finally meet you! The girls talk about you all the time."

María raised an eyebrow at Cora.

"I hope they say good things! It's nice to meet you as well. Sofía has told us all about your daughter Janelle."

The girls punctuated María's sentence with a joyful shriek as they played.

"I'll let y'all go. I'm sure you have a lot of prep work to host both your families tonight. I just wanted to come say hey and introduce myself. Y'all holler if you need anything!"

As quickly as she had come to talk to us, she walked back to her porch where Marianne still sat. She waved at them and went back to watching the kids run around in the yard.

"I guess that's our cue to get cooking!" Cora said with a sigh. "You ready to go inside?"

"I am ready to be warm again," María told her, then offered the shorter woman her arm. "Come on. Let's get back into the heat."

~

Chapter 3

BY THE TIME Elena and her brothers arrived back at the house, Cora felt like the entire house was in chaos. Three different timers were going off in the kitchen and Sofía and David were running around talking at what seemed like the highest possible volume.

The kitchen was normally comfortable for her and Elena. With all of the Mendézes in it, and all of the food on the counters, Cora was fairly certain that there wasn't a single square inch of space left unused in the room. And then the doorbell rang.

"I get it!" David yelled in his highest pitched voice. Cora glanced at the stove and saw that it was nearly 4 PM, which meant that the people ringing the doorbell were her parents.

Their timing, as usual, could not have been worse. Cora heard her mother's voice talking to the two-year-old and called out to them.

"Come on in, guys! I'm in the kitchen!"

She shoved the oven mitts back onto her hands and grabbed a pot of boiling potatoes by both handles.

"Coming through!" Cora shouted, making her way through the crush of people and trying to avoid burning them with the outside of the pot. The colander was waiting in the sink and she dumped the soft potatoes into it.

Steam billowed up from the sink, clouding around her face. She turned quickly, coughing at the sudden, intense smell of potatoes. When she opened her eyes, her parents were standing in the arched doorway of the kitchen.

Her mother wore a simple and elegant maroon tea length dress that hugged her slight curves, and her father wore a pale green buttoned shirt with a tie that matched his wife's dress. hey each held a few presents, and had matching nervous smiles plastered on their faces.

Elena tapped Cora's mother on the shoulder from behind, a genuinely welcoming expression on her face. Both parents turned and Cora lost sight of their expressions.

"It's so good to see you, Victoria!" Elena cried, wrapping Cora's mother in a gentle hug.

"Hugh and I are always glad to see you, Elena," Victoria reminded her as Cora's father offered his best handshake.

That was all the Cora could hear over the din of the kitchen, but she watched Elena led them into the living room to put down the presents.

Turning back to the sink full of steaming potatoes, Cora lifted the colander by its handles and shook it until there was no water left in them.

"Gabriel, can you help me out?" she called over my shoulder. "Get the bowl ready for these, would you?"

"Already there! Just bring them over."

Cora did as she was asked and stepped back. Gabriel

took over, mixing the cream cheese, sour cream, and chives into the potatoes and began mashing. She wiped her forehead on her shoulder.

She couldn't believe how hot it was in the kitchen with all of the various appliances running, not to mention Elena's brothers and mother in the room.

As if summoned by Cora's thoughts, María appeared next to her, spiriting the young white woman out of her own kitchen.

"Go spend time with your mother," María commanded her. "We've got it handled in here."

Cora had every intention of following her instructions until she asked her to wait.

"You'll do better if you change into your Christmas clothes, my girl. Your parents will be more impressed."

As usual, María was right. The close the Cora was wearing now were splattered with various things that she had been cooking and cleaning since she had returned home from shopping. She hadn't even thought about changing before greeting her parents, but it was a good idea.

She had picked the perfect green dress for tonight, complete with a cardigan and pockets that would allow her to conceal the ring in her pocket and keep her warm, which was always a priority.

Family was a source of anxiety for Cora, but she always felt better when she looked good, and her mother liked it when she wore dresses. She hoped the outfit would earn her a few brownie points.

Cora pressed a kiss to Maria's floury cheek and walked back to the office to change. Elena had warned her this morning that she wasn't going to be allowed into the bedroom because she had to put some finishing touches on Cora's Christmas presents.

Cora knew better than to argue with her about it, so she'd planned ahead. She slid out of her food-splattered clothes, tossing them into the laundry basket with a sigh.

The dress slid easily off of the hanger, thanks to the satin lining on the interior. She loved the way that the satin lining felt against her skin as she stepped into it. It was a beautiful dress that she rarely had an opportunity to wear, and it was the perfect armor against her anxiety about what might or might not come out of her parent's mouths during the festivities.

They weren't terrible people, but they were older and fairly privileged, which meant they didn't always think about the effect of what they were saying before they spoke. It was the first time that Cora had introduced her parents to a female partner's family, and she couldn't help but be nervous.

She took a deep breath in through her nose for fortification before returning into the fray of the household. It smelled perfectly wonderful in the house between all of the different dishes that were still being put together in the kitchen. She closed her office door behind her, hoping to keep the children out of it, and found herself wishing that Luis was making coquito that was as rummy as Elena liked it. She also wished that was a healthy way to handle strained relationships, instead of just a delicious way to get drunk. She just had to make it through the evening and she would be okay, she told herself.

Cora heard laughter echoing from the living room, and was a little stunned by what she saw. Sofia and David were crawling all over her parents, and the normally uptight couple were smiling at them.

She plastered a happy smile onto her face and sauntered into the room

"Hiya, folks! I see you're already making friends."

"Cora, darling! You didn't tell me that these children would be so delightful!" her mother exclaimed.

Elena sat in the wide armchair next to them, watching the children carefully to make sure they didn't grab onto the Christmas tree on the other side of Hugh. Cora caught her eye and Elena raised an eyebrow at her that says that it was going well. She tried starting a conversation again.

"So how was the drive up, Dad? Hit any traffic?"

"Oh, not any more than we expected," Dad said, waving a hand at Cora. "You know the ride from Raleigh here is nothing to be worried about. There's rarely more than two or three cars on the road."

"There weren't even any tractors on the road this time, right, Hugh? That was a nice change!"

"I'd have been more concerned if there were tractors on the road on Christmas Eve, Victoria." He looked seriously at Victoria, who waggled her eyebrows at him like a cartoon villain. Cora smile became a little less forced their antics.

Well, here's to hoping the rest of this evening goes this well, she thought to herself.

A SLIGHTLY SWEET, yet meaty, smell was floating out of the oven, telling everyone in the house that it was time to eat before the last timer went off.

María and Victoria worked together to arrange the various dishes on the counter so that everyone could get to everything while the meat cooled enough for Manuel to slice it up for eating.

Looking at the ham, Cora realized that she might

have gotten a little too much meat for the size of their party. A 20-pound ham may have been overkill, but they would have plenty of leftovers to enjoy for the next week. That wouldn't be a problem.

So far, all of their families were getting along swimmingly. Cora hadn't heard a single political argument or even a rowdy discussion that hadn't dissolved into laughter. Sofía and David had been running in and out all day, and Cora thought she had spotted Janelle's small afro outside with them the living room window. Everyone seems to be having a great time, even Cora, despite her nerves. She hoped that stuffing herself full of food would help quash the rest of her anxiety, as it usually did.

All of the smells of the various foods they had made mingled in the air together, creating a cacophony of scent that nobody could resist.

Cora was pretty sure that there had never been this much food in their house at once. Bowls and serving platters overflowed with all kinds of delicious foods, from the mashed potatoes to the green bean casserole, and the macaroni and cheese they'd made for the kids. Mac & cheese was always a safe bet for picky eaters like Cora herself and the kids who were unwilling to try new things.

As they laid out the table, Cora kept catching herself fidgeting with the ring box that she was hiding in her dress pocket. She was grateful that Elena was sitting across from her instead of next to her. Being able to look her in her beautiful face would hopefully distract her from the ring that felt like it was burning a hole in her pocket.

Hugh and Manuel worked together to slice enough

of the ham for everyone to eat, splitting it between two platters for the table.

Finally, all that was left was for someone to lead the two families in prayer. Cora's family had given the honor to Elena's family, since the Moss's were not particularly religious. Cora was interested to see what kind of prayer the Mendézes would use, since they were all practicing Catholics.

"Everybody, take your seats, and take the hands of the person sitting next to you," Gabriel announced to the room. The chatter in the room hushed as everyone dashed to their places.

"We're holding hands for two reasons. The first is because we're family and because I said so. The second is because I don't trust any of y'all not to steal bites of food while we're not looking."

Everyone laughed. Once everyone was in their seats, Gabriel told them to bow their heads.

"Lord, thank you for giving us all the health and happiness to enjoy this blessed holiday as a family," Gabriel said earnestly. "I pray that we may all be filled with the wonder of Mary, the joy of the angels, the eagerness of the shepherds, the determination of the magi, and the peace of your son Jesus Christ throughout these days and the year to come. May the Almighty God, Father, Son, and Holy Spirit bless us all, now and forever."

All of the voices in the room came together as a chorus of amen's, and slowly, everyone released the hands of the people on either side of them.

"Now, let's eat!" Gabriel hollered. The kids cheered.

No one in the room needed to be told twice. Marianne and Anton sprung into action, making plates for the kids first.

They had a rule that the kids had to try a bite of everything that they hadn't tried before, which led to the kids having some very weird favorite foods. Cora couldn't wait to get her own plate started. She was starving.

ACROSS THE TABLE, Elena was fidgeting with her dress and the tablecloth. Adelaide had dropped off the dog right before they left for their own family gathering, and Elena had hidden her in the bedroom while Cora was putting the finishing touches on the ham.

Before each place setting sat a colorful paper cylinder that was wrapped like candy. Elena wasn't sure what would come out of them, but it was sure to be a fun surprise. Christmas crackers were something that her family had never really done but were a tradition in Cora's. The kids had never seen them before and were happily sword fighting with them from across the card table that they'd set up as the kid's table. It was adorable.

Once everyone had their plates, Cora got the table's attention.

"Okay, so I know not everybody has done Christmas records before, so I thought we'd give a little tutorial. It's super simple, but I didn't want to confuse anyone. Everybody takes one end of the cracker in their hands and the person next to them takes the other end. On the count of three, both people pull and out pops a bunch of toys and stuff!"

"Yay toys! Mama, I want toys!" David interrupted. Everyone at the table laughed.

"Well, I guess we're all ready then! Let's go!"

She took her seat across the table from Elena and

presented one end of her cylinder to Papí and the other to her father. Elena handed hers to Mama and Victoria.

"Okay, let's count together!" She called and glanced around the table. "One! Two! Three!"

Everyone pulled on the cylinders, and they released their contents in a chorus of pops. Paper confetti, silicone toys, and paper hats sprayed across the table, landing in each of the plates.

"Oh, now there's confetti in the food! I... did not think that through. I'm so sorry, everybody!"

She clasped her hands together tightly in what Elena knew was worry as their families began picking the larger chunks of confetti and toys out. Mama and Papí didn't bother, simply

"What's a little extra fiber in our diets?" Hugh said with a wink. Cora rolled her eyes at her father, but stopped wringing her hands together. Everyone simply picked out what they could and began eating around the rest.

Elena looked inside her own cracker and saw that there was still some paper on the inside. She pulled out and saw that it was a paper crown. She knew exactly what she was going to do with it

"Mama, give me your head."

María turned to her, confused, until Elena placed the flimsy crown on her mother's head.

"There! Now you are the queen we always knew you were!"

Papí and Cora laughed, and Mama beamed back at Elena.

ONCE THEY HAD BEGUN EATING, Elena had to resist the urge to go back and check on the dog every few minutes. Her brothers had that well in hand. Every so often, one of them would excuse themselves to go to the bathroom and make sure that she was okay and stayed quiet. So far, she thought, so good.

Elena was having a great time with her family. Luís had just started a job at a new accounting firm and seemed to be enjoying it. She'd even gotten to share some funny stories from her own coworkers at the law firm.

Mr. Sturgess, her boss, was an absolute character and tended to hire people that complemented his own strangeness. Victoria and Hugh had not believed her when she told him about his annual Halloween costume until Cora had broken out the pictures that they took together. The table was roaring with laughter. Tears were streaming down Papi's face, and even Victoria had laughed out loud. It was a rare sight, but Elena was happy that she had brought them all together, at least for a little bit. She knew that Cora had been incredibly anxious about how her parents would act when dealing with the entire Mendéz family at once for the first time.

Elena wasn't sure exactly how they had managed to be dating for this long without their families having come together. It seemed like one of her brothers visited their house once a week, but they could never manage to get the whole family together when Victoria and Hugh could join them. To be fair, Cora's parents did live much further away than Elena's did. It was less convenient for them to visit frequently.

Marianne shouted a little bit in surprise. The rest of the table looked over. Anton was giggling a high pitched, slightly horrified giggle. Elena looked at her sister in law and saw why. Sofía had spat her mouthful of brussel sprouts all over her mother's face. Marianne's mouth hung open in surprise, the sauteed vegetables leaving a trail of butter and garlic behind them. as they slid down her brown face.

"Are you okay, Marianne?" María asked, trying to hold back a laugh of her own from down the table.

Luís, seated next to her, handed her a napkin which she took with trembling fingers. Elena didn't think she'd ever seen Marianne look so offended as she wiped off the remnants of the sprouts-and her makeup.

"Okay, we're adding brussel sprouts to the 'no' list, then," Anton quipped once he managed to stop giggling at his wife's face.

"Ya think?"

At that, the entire table burst into laughter. Marianne joined in after a moment, her laugh sounding like small bells. Without a thought, Anton took over helping David with his plate. Sofía, uncaring about the commotion in the room, was chowing down on the foods she actually liked on her plate.

Marianne excused herself to the restroom to see if she could salvage her makeup. Elena was fairly certain that she would also be checking on the puppy in the bedroom. Once David's food was sliced up and ready to eat, Anton turned back to his daughter.

"Now, Sofía, what did we say about eating food you didn't like?" Elena could tell by the tone of his voice that he was staring at his nine-year-old sternly.

"To spit it out!" Sofía replied cheerfully, putting another bite of food in her mouth.

She watched him rub his hands through his hair before focusing on his daughter.

"To spit it out where, mi hija?"

"…into my napkin."

"Into your napkin. Which you did not do just now."

Sofía played with her food contritely.

"I forgot, Papa. I'm sorry."

"Don't apologize to me. I'm not the one you spit food all over. You owe your mother some extra love and apologies tonight."

"I'll be extra good, Papa, I promise."

"I believe it. Now eat your dinner."

She didn't have to be told twice.

Chapter 4

SOFÍA AND DAVID were nearly falling asleep in their plates as the adults finished their meals. Elena was fairly certain that Papí wouldn't be far behind them. Mama was the only one who wasn't starting to droop when Cora spoke up.

"We have a tradition in our family," Cora said hesitantly. Her parents perked up at the mention, trading excited glances with each other.

"You suffered through ours like a champ," Anton said with a wink. "What's your tradition?"

Victoria spoke up, to everyone's surprise.

"When Cora was little, we used to take her to her grandmother's house for Christmas every year. There wasn't a whole lot for her to do there, but she insisted on staying up all night anyway to meet Santa Claus!"

The whole table laughed, and Cora's ears turned pink.

"Anyway, we started allowing her to open one present on Christmas Eve from one of her cousins, to help entertain her while she stayed up. I didn't know if maybe your young ones might want to do the same thing, since we are spending the night in a hotel?"

That got the kids' attention.

"Presents!" Sofia cried happily, clapping her hands together. "Papa I want to do presents!"

The table erupted into more laughter.

"Well, I guess that settles it, doesn't it? Let's leave the dishes for when the kids are occupied, shall we?"

"You're going to have to roll me to the living room," Hugh said, rubbing his hand over his belly happily. Luís, who was already standing, playfully tipped the older man's chair to the side, as if to make him roll. It startled the nervous gasp from him and Victoria, but the gas quickly turned into a laugh when he caught sight of the wide grin on her brothers face.

Luís offered his hand to Cora's dad, who took it with a grin of his own.

"Thanks, son."

Elena caught Cora watching her parents with soft eyes, something that was rare for her. She couldn't help but notice just how beautiful her girlfriend was, feeling a goofy smile spread across her own face as she stared.

Cora caught her staring and crossed her eyes in a silly expression. Elena replied by sticking her tongue out, and Cora laughed a laugh that sent tingles up Elena's spine.

"All right, everybody, make your way to the living room!" She began herding the kids across the hallway, like it was the most natural thing in the world. Elena could hear her making Sofia into her partner in crime as they made their way into the living room. "Now, Sofia. Since you're the oldest, you'll have to help your brother pick out the presents that are for him. Can you do that?"

Her childish response was muffled, but Elena

grinned. It was time to bring out the first of her surprises.

WITH THE REST of their family members trying to find somewhere to sit in the living room, it was easy for Elena to sneak back to the bedroom. She found Janelle and Adelaide sitting on the floor next to the open crate, which explained why she had been so quiet during dinner.

In fact, the room was nearly silent except for the sounds of Adelaide tapping out messages on her phone and all three of them breathing. She breathed it in while she stood inside the closed doorway, counting her blessings.

"Thank you so much for watching over her today. I could not have made this the surprise it will be without you two.

The dog was laying in the crate that her foster parents had given them, her small white head laying on her tiny, well-trimmed paws. Even the biggest dog hater would have to admit that she was absolutely adorable, and Elena was not that.

Her full name was to be Lady Georgina Robertson the Third. It was perfectly pretentious enough for this beautiful dog and had easy nickname potential. Plus, it was the name that Cora had always said she would name her first dog. Elena had never been able to figure out where the Third part came from, but she rolled with it. The evening had gone beautifully so far and she couldn't wait to see the surprise on Cora's face when she met her.

"Hey, sweetie," Elena said, smiling softly at the small dog in her crate. She really was cute.

Her ears lifted slightly, and her tail wagged, as if she knew what Elena was thinking. That, or she saw the leash in her hand. Elena suspected it was a mix of the two.

"Are you ready to meet your Mama, my lady?"

That got her tail wagging for real, and Elena grinned. Georgina let Elena clip the thin red leash to the small holly-patterned harness Luís had bought her on a whim. She looked very festive. All she needed was a little bow, and she'd look just like a Christmas present.

Luckily, Elena was prepared. She tied Luís's other purchase - a ribbon - into a bow around her neck like a collar, straightening it so that the large bowl was at the back of her head and so that the loops did not touch her ears.

Luís had mentioned that she hadn't liked it when the groomer's messed with them, and Elena didn't want her to be any more uncomfortable than she had to be, especially with so many people around.

Elena took a deep breath to fortify herself for the excitement and noise that she knew was coming and opened the door. The hinge squeaked, announcing their presence as they walked out.

Georgina padded ahead of her into the hallway, making barely any sound on the hardwood floors. Cora's mother leaned against the living room's arched doorway. She was the first to notice the new addition to the household, her pink lips forming an 'oh' of surprise.

Elena pressed a finger to her lips, hoping that Victoria wouldn't spoil the moment. She was as big a fan of small dogs as her daughter was, and tended to be a little bit more dramatic than necessary.

"Get Cora," Elena mouthed as noiselessly as

possible. Victoria nodded, and waved to get her daughter's attention.

"Darling, there's something you should see out here!" she called. Lady Georgina, apparently sensing the moment, sat between Elena's feet. Her short tail swished back and forth between her ankles happily while they waited for Cora to climb out of the press of people.

Elena heard Cora ask Victoria what she wanted, and saw Victoria gesture to where she stood. Cora turned and nearly screamed with joy.

"Oh my God," she yelped. "Oh my God!"

Her mom shushed her, and Cora knelt on the ground.

"Hi, sweetie."

She used a soothing tone, and Lady Georgina reacted to it, walking forward quickly to sniff her face and hands. The dog jumped up, her paws connecting with Cora's shoulders. She giggled, then coughed.

"Tongue in my mouth!" she laughed. "What's your name, sweet lady?"

Her mom's eyes were wide, and she had to laugh loudly when Elena said the name out loud.

"It's the perfect name," she said between laughs. "she looks so prim and proper! Oh, Hugh, you've gotta see this!"

Cora's dad poked his head out of the doorway, and his face split into a wide grin at the sight of his daughter kneeling in front of a dog who was very excitedly licking her face.

"Well, Vic, it looks like we became grandparents a little earlier than planned."

He boomed a laugh into the hall, which got Elena's family's attention. Elena pulled lightly on Lady Georgina's leash, just enough to get her off of Cora's shoulders. She worried slightly that the dog would be freaked out by the kids and accidentally bite someone out of fright.

"Papa, there's a doggie!" Sofia announced once she made it into the hallway with us. "Can I pet it?"

"I don't think she's ready to be petted yet, mi vida. She needs to get used to Tía Cora and Elena first, okay? But you can wave to her!"

Sofia accepted this, waving furiously at the little white dog. David followed her lead, waving so hard he nearly fell over. Cora's gaze lingered on Lady Georgina and Elena smiled at how happy she looked.

She rose from the floor, her knees creaking as she did so. She made her way towards Elena, who caught the full force of her loving gaze. It took her breath away.

She wrapped her arms around her girlfriend and pressed a soft, wet kiss to her cheek.

"Thank you for being my best family," Cora whispered in her ear. "And for expanding it to include the sweetest little dog."

CORA

Elena's brothers set up a baby gate that was left over from Sophia and David's younger days to keep the dog out of the kitchen and living room while the kids were in the house.

None of them wanted her to get into any of the Christmas presents or the Tupperware that were still sitting on the counters in the kitchen, but they didn't want her to be locked in her crate, either. It was a good compromise that allowed her to explore the house while everyone else did Christmas things and avoided stressing her out before she had a chance to get used to her new environment.

The families resettled into the living room, where the kids and María would be getting presents. They hadn't intended on giving Elena's mother one of her present early, but the children had insisted on giving their present to her early, too. Who were they to deny María a gift early when it would make the kid's happy?

It had been decided that Luís, as both the smallest of the siblings and the one who had done most of the organizing, would be the one hunting for the presents under the tree. He was happily ensconced in the tree's large lower branches, passing boxes out as he found them.

The gift for David from Gabriel and Luís was the largest box under the tree, while the gift that Elena and Cora had gotten for Sofía was much smaller. Cora was a little uncomfortable with that dynamic, but toys for two-year-olds were always so much bigger than toys for preteens. They had a lot more things for Sofía than they did for David overall. Plus, she knew that they would both absolutely love their gifts, and that's what really counted.

Luís emerged with a gift bag that Cora recognized as one that they had given to Anton the year prior. She and Elena made eye contact across the room and smirked at each other.

"Okay! Here's Mama's gift!"

He handed it to her where she sat snuggled on the loveseat with Manuel. Cora loved how touchy they always were with each other. Even though they spent the whole day together, Manuel had his arms around María's waist, and she had her head tilted towards him.

It was just wonderful to see how in love but they still were even after so many years together.

Cora glanced at her own parents, who were standing in the doorway still. Even though they stood on opposite sides of the arched doorway, their hands were just barely linked together.

"Can we open them now?" Sofia asked loudly, realizing that not enough people were paying attention to her for her liking. Her parents laughed, and the rest of the room joined in.

"Go for it, but help your brother first," Marianne told her.

She rolled her eyes, but did as she was told. She wasn't about to disobey her mother after spitting brussel sprouts at her. She spread her fingers out like a cat's claws and pulled them across the shiny gold-and-white striped wrapping paper, tearing it away from the box that was larger than her younger brother.

"It's a truck!" David yelled in delight once he helped his sister pull all of the paper. "It's a big truck for me!"

"Yeah, buddy! Tomorrow, you can ride it around in the yard! What do you think, David?" Gabriel asked.

"That is awesome! Can sissy ride with me?"

"I think so! But not until tomorrow, okay? And only outside."

"Okay!" He pushed the box out into the hallway, making truck and vroom sounds with his mouth as he moved it. Marianne grinned at him from across the room.

"Now it's your turn, Sofia," Anton told her.

She ripped into her own gift box and looked up with a confused expression when she pulled out a banana-shaped cloth bag.

"What is this?"

"It's a game called Bananagrams! You get a handful of letters and you have to make words out of it."

Her eyes lit up and Cora smiled.

"That sounds fun! How do you win?"

Cora laughed.

"You have to make the most words out of everybody you're playing with. It's one of my favorites."

"Can we play now?"

Her mother intervened.

"How about you, Papa, and I play when we get back to the hotel? It's getting late for David to be up and you can play with Tía Cora tomorrow. How's that sound?"

David interrupted, to Cora's amusement.

"But Mama, I don't wanna go to bed yet! I wanna see Santa!"

"Santa doesn't come if you aren't sleeping, David. You know that!" Sofia informed him haughtily. The room lit up with laughter, and he frowned.

"That's right," Anton told him patiently. "The sooner that you go to bed, the sooner Santa can come and give you the rest of your presents."

"Then I want to go to bed now, please." David unintentionally punctuated his sentence with the wide yawn that stretched his chubby face.

"We'll go home soon, mi hijo," Marianne explained. "We have to give Abuela her present first. Do you want to help her open it?"

His box abandoned, David scrambled over to where his grandparents sat and up onto María's lap. She handed him the gift bag and he tugged the tissue paper out with the reckless abandon that only a two-year-old could find. He lifted a bright blue apron out of the bag and frowned at it with his entire face.

"¿Qué dice, abuela?"

María smiled down at him.

"It says 'Kiss the Cook!'" she read with a laugh.

"Who am I to deny the apron?" Manuel announced, then pressed a kiss to his wife's lips. She kissed him back.

"Gross! I don't like kissing!" David shouted, and scrambled away from his grandparents. "We can leave now!"

The entire room burst into laughter. María and Manuel broke apart after a moment, both of their cheeks flushing just a little. Cora winked at them, and María mouthed back a thank you.

Chapter 5

CORA AND ELENA stood in the doorway of their home, watching and waving to their families as they loaded into the cars. They would be back in the morning, but their house was not large enough to host everyone overnight, so they were off to the hotel to sleep.

Both women have a long day and felt relief at the quiet that was all around them, aside from Lady Georgina's energetic sniffing in the bedroom.

"It feels like it might snow," Elena remarked, rubbing her hands gently up and down Cora's cardigan-clad arms. Cora nodded, nestling closer against her. The three cars were pulling out of the driveway and headed for their hotels, and it was cold on the freshly shaved back and sides of her head. "Let's head back in before we freeze out here."

"How do you feel about lighting a fire?" Cora asked hopefully. She felt Elena's chest move with a quiet laugh.

The working fireplace had been one of the biggest draws for this house for the both of them, but it was Cora's favorite. There was very little that she loved more than the sound of a crackling fire and the smell of cedar smoke in the winter.

She could happily curl up with the book and a blanket on the couch and be completely content for an entire evening.

"A fire sounds lovely, along with a glass of wine," Elena said. "Come on. Let's get you back into pajamas like I know you want to be."

She walked back inside, sliding her shoes off and leaving them at the door. Cora followed suit, closing and locking the door behind her. The floor was warm against her bare feet.

"I'm actually quite comfortable in this dress," Cora told Elena. "C'mon. You get the wine and let the dog out here. I'll get the fire started, and then I have a present for you."

She raised a thick eyebrow at Cora, barely pausing in her way towards the kitchen.

"I thought you said that all of my presents needed to be opened tomorrow."

"I lied. I've been known to do that from time to time, but only for a good cause."

"And is this a good cause?"

Cora grinned toothily at her girlfriend.

"It is."

Elena shook her head at Cora, her dark hair cascading down her shoulders. A wide smile split her face as she walked into the kitchen to get the wine glasses and red wine we'd been saving.

Cora walked in the opposite direction, working to clear space around the fireplace in the living room. They had a policy of always leaving the fireplace ready to go - a fire starter made of dryer lint and a toilet paper roll, two or three logs and a little bit of kindling.

She lifted the long-nosed lighter from the mantelpiece and squatted before the fire. She laid the lighter's nose against the firestarter. With a click, flame burst from the end and it caught with a whoosh.

Cora pulled the metal gates closed in front of the flickering flame, hoping to keep it where they belonged and everything else out of its space - particularly our new family member.

She heard Elena's footsteps coming across the hall, her left ankle popping the third step, followed by shuffling patter of doggy footsteps. Cora still couldn't believe that they had a dog, especially this one. She had always loved small dogs, especially West Highland Terriers, though she wasn't entirely sure why.

"Hey, buddy," she crooned, her voice several octaves higher than normal when the dog trotted into view in front of Elena. She shifted her gaze upward and saw a smile on Elena's face. Her voice dropped to its usual pitch. "Hey, beautiful."

Lady Georgina showed no hesitancy as she wandered around the room. She sniffed her way over to where Cora sat, her small pink tongue hanging out of the side of her mouth. Elena watched her carefully, making sure she did get into anything that she shouldn't. That was when Cora noticed that Elena had the glasses and bottle of wine that she had sent her for. With a groan, Cora rose to her feet.

Elena set the wine glasses on the coffee table and began wrestling with the cork. Cora reached down and allowed Georgina to sniff her hand as much as she pleased.

Despite knowing the sound was coming, Cora jumped at the sound of the cork popping out of the bottle. They both laughed at her response. Elena poured the wine into the two glasses, making sure not to overfill them or slosh the plum colored liquid onto the soft white rug they stood on.

Cora couldn't help but be amazed at how graceful she was.

"Let's toast!" Elena said. "To our first family Christmas Eve being a success, and to tomorrow going just as welll!"

"I'll drink to that!" Cora answered cheerfully, clinking her glass against Elena's gently. Elena leaned over and kissed her gently.

Cora licked her lips, savoring the taste of her girlfriend's soft lips and the waxy residue from her warm red lipstick that remained on her own lips. They smiled softly at each other over their wine glasses and drank.

The 2015 vintage was fruity. Cora could taste plum and raspberry, with hints of something floral. It was lightly spiced, and it was delicious. Once Elena had swallowed her sip, she looked coyly at her.

"Now, you said you had a present for me."

"Indeed I did!"

Cora set her wine glass on the coffee table, far enough in that she didn't think the dog would be able to reach it. Her hands were starting to shake, and she didn't want Elena to see just how nervous she was when she got down on one knee.

I really hope I'm not about to ruin Christmas forever, Cora thought desperately before pulling the small box out of her pocket.

"Elena MaríaMendéz, you are the light of my life. Every day spent with you is the day that I wouldn't trade for anything in any galaxy. I don't want there to be a part of my life that you were not in. "

Elena gasped, but Cora kept going. She was already

crying, but she hadn't managed to get the actual question out of her mouth yet. She popped open the box to show Elena the three-banded rose gold ring that she had bought her. The hand that wasn't holding her wine glass flew to her mouth at the sight of it.

"Will you agree to spend this slice of eternity by my side and be my wife?"

She looked up at Elena, tears spilling down her face. Elena's eyes were brimming with tears of her own, but her lips were spread in a wide, quivering grin.

"Oh, stay there for a moment. Don't move. I'll be right back."

She set her wine glass down next to Cora's, then ran toward the back of the house. Cora watched her go, utterly bewildered. That was not the response that she had expected when she proposed, and she wasn't entirely sure it was a positive one.

She was, however, glad that she hadn't put on any mascara or eyeliner. If she had, it would've been running down her face horribly. She wiped her eyes and opened them again to see Elena slide back into the living room.

She raised her hand and Cora saw that she held a box similar to Cora's own in it. It was Cora's turn to gasp as Elena got down on one knee in front of her.

"I had planned to do this tomorrow morning," Elena said with a laugh, sliding the ribbon off of her own box and opening it. She couldn't even look at the ring because of the joy radiating from her face. "Cora Elise Moss, I promise to love you for every single day that God allows us to spend together. I promise to always cherish you and our love above all else in this world, if you will do me the honor of being my wife."

They knelt in silence for a moment, both crying and

grinning before bursting into laughter and leaning towards each other.

"Yes, absolutely yes," she told Cora.

Cora reached her arms out to Elena, wrapping them around the love of her life. She gave her own reply in a whisper.

"I will say yes to you every single day of the rest of my life."

They stayed on the floor like that for a long time, until Georgina poked her cold nose into Elena's thigh. Elena jumped, and both women giggled. Elena leaned back on her haunches, petting the dog lightly along its back.

"Well, let's put these rings on, shall we, my love?"

ELENA

She could not believe how well tonight had gone. Elena's heart was so full, and it raced so quickly that she thought it might burst out of her chest.

Cora held out the ring box to her, and she was gratified to notice that Cora's small, pale hand was shaking as much as her own was. She also realized that she had been so caught up with her counter-proposal that she hadn't even looked at the ring that Cora had proposed with.

Taking the box, Elena was stunned. It looked like someone had taken the lines of a sweetheart neckline and turned it into a ring. Three crystal-encrusted bands came together in the center with a gently-sloping V with slightly larger clear stones in them.

"Oh, Cora, this is beautiful!" Elena breathed. "What are the stones?"

Cora slid the ring onto Elena's hand, and she was surprised by how warm it was.

"Oh good. Then you'll like the one I bought you, too."

Cora laughed quietly. Georgina had made her way over to the couch, climbed up and gone to sleep. The small dog snored lightly a few feet away from the two women.

Elena picked up the ring box she'd proposed with and held it out to her with a trembling smile.

"I will love you to the ends of the universe and back," Elena told Cora, sliding the galactic ring onto her ring finger while the sound of the fire crackled around them.

She gasped at the sight of it. She clearly hadn't really looked at the ring, either.

Elena looked into her face, which was just below mine her own, and realized that tears were spilling down her face again as she looked at her hand. Elena cupped Cora's wet cheeks in her hands and pressed a kiss to her mouth.

Cora leaned into the kiss, and Elena felt her nip lightly at her lips. Elena was pretty sure that she would never get over how much she loved the feel of Cora's lips on hers. Her heart begin to race, and she could feel from where one of her palms had slid down to her neck that hers was as well.

"I love you so much," Cora choked out, before tears overwhelmed her. She wrapped her arms around Elena's neck and collapsed into the larger woman. Elena slipped her arms around Cora's waist, pulling her as close as was physically possible on the deep pile rug.

Neither woman could have told anyone how long they sat there holding each other. It was long enough that Lady Georgina woke up and came to join them at Cora's feet, jolting them back into reality with her cool, wet nose.

"How about we head to bed, darling?"

Cora tilted her head back to smile at Elena.

"Bed sounds perfect."

ELENA

Cora and Elena pulled all of the presents out of the office to make a big impact on the kids when they arrived. However, they were sure that the presents would not be the only things making an impact, and they weren't disappointed.

Squeals of joy split the early morning air in our home when both of their families arrived for Christmas morning, just like the matching grins of delight that split Cora and Elena's faces.

Cora's mother burst into tears at the sight of the rings on their fingers. Hugh wrapped Elena up in a bone-crushing hug that Victoria joined in on, turning her into a Moss sandwich.

"Welcome to the family officially, my darling."

As soon as Elena was free from their crushing hug, Sofía grabbed Elena's left hand in both of her tiny ones. She peered and squinted at the ring very seriously.

"It looks like a butterfly," she declared. "I like it."

Elena looked down at the ring on her hand and realized delightedly that she was right. The V in the center almost looked like antennas, and the arched rose gold bands could be mistaken for a butterfly's wings.

"Go tell Cora you like it," Elena told her. Lowering her voice to a conspiratorial whisper, she continued. "And check out the one I had made for her. I think you'll like that one, too."

She let out a peal of laughter and ran over to where Cora stood in the kitchen with Elena's parents.

"Tía Cora! Tía Cora! Lemme see!" Sofía

Elena looked up just as the little girl grabbed Cora's hand the same way she had done with Elena's. Cora's giggle filled my ears from across the room, and Elena grinned.

She couldn't have wished for a more perfect morning, and they hadn't even eaten yet. Everything was perfect.

THE END

The Ghosts of Halloween

A Learning Curves Short Story Collection

Ceillie Simkiss

Cover: Ceillie Simkiss

Halloween is a holiday that is both loved and reviled by people all over America. It's one of Cora's favorite holidays. Unfortunately, it's also a massive source of anxiety for Elena. Between the two of them, they get up to all sorts of hijinks and wind up falling even more head over heels for each other in The Ghosts of Halloween.

The Ghosts of Halloween collection is made up of three sweet slice-of-life short stories: Past, Present and Future. Each tells the story of a different Halloween that Cora and Elena have gone or will go through together.

Past:

Cora forgets about a planned Halloween party she's supposed to attend with Elena. Will she make it in time for the festivities?

Present:

Elena gets a surprise invitation to her new job's Halloween party – and costumes are mandatory. Will they come up with appropriate costumes in time for the party?

Future:

Five years after the events of Learning Curves, Elena takes her niblings trick-or-treating.

The Ghosts of Halloween is a continuation of the Learning Curves series, but can be read as a standalone collection featuring the lesbian and asexual characters from the original stories.

∼

Halloween Past

CORA HAD no idea how long she had been working when her phone vibrated, disrupting her workflow. Elena's face popped up on the screen, and she swiped to answer it quickly.

"Good evening, light of my life!" Cora sang into the phone, compulsively saving her document. "How are you today?"

"Hey, babe. Where are you?"

Cora froze in her office chair. She went through her mental calendar, trying to figure out where she was supposed to be. She realized what day it was and slapped a hand to her forehead.

"*Fuck!*"

"Cora, I reminded you about the party this morning. Did you forget already?"

She could hear the exasperation in her girlfriend's voice, and hated that she was the reason it was there.

"I was working on that article I'm writing and I got completely tied up. I'm so sorry. Let me save what I'm doing and I'll be there!"

Elena huffed at her.

"Need me to text you the address?"

"Yes please?"

"Okay, let me know when you're on your way, please?"

"Of course. I'll see you soon. Love you."

"Love you, too," Elena muttered before hanging up.

She set the phone down on her desk, saving her file again before closing it, cursing herself both internally and externally. Cora could not believe she had forgot about this party - Elena had been talking about it for at least two weeks. Cora was fuzzy on the details about the party, but she knew it was important to Elena that she be there, and she'd completely lost track of time.

"Goddamn hyperfocus," she berated herself. "Why didn't I set an alarm for myself to get ready?"

She dove into her closet to find the pieces of her costume, glad that she had at least planned this far ahead. She could only imagine how pissed Elena would be if she hadn't prepared a costume at all. She hadn't done much for Halloween the last few years. Since it fell so close to her birthday, almost all of her childhood birthday parties had been costumed, and she had been a little burnt out on them after undergrad.

However, there was very little that she wouldn't do for Elena - and she wanted her at this party, so Cora would be there.

"Now where are those boots…" she mumbled.

She dropped to her hands and knees, trying to find the chunky heeled black boots she intended to wear. Digging past the sneakers and flip flops that littered the floor, she found them, all the way in the back corner. She got them out, and groaned. A thin film of dust covered the leather. She couldn't remember when last she'd worn them, and now she realized it must have been even longer than she'd thought. She hoped they still fit.

She threw the boots over to the bed in annoyance, and rose to her feet. She grabbed the hanger that held the rest of her costume - a orange knit sweater and Red pixie pants that would tuck into the boots perfectly. Together with the round-rimmed glasses she now needed to wear, and the curly bob that her hair had grown into, it would make the perfect Velma costume.

Her other option had been cutting holes into an old sheet and being what Elena called a "basic ass ghost," but that had sounded cold, so she had decided against it. There was nothing worse than being cold *and* uncomfortable. The Velma costume would be much more comfortable in the long run, and she wasn't sure how long this party was going last. Comfort was key.

She tossed the hanger onto the bed and scrambled into the bathroom to find a way to clean the boots. Casting her glance around the room, she settled on grabbing a makeup remover wipe.

That ought to do nicely, she thought. She hurriedly wiped the boots down, and tossed the wipe into the overflowing trash can by her desk. She really needed to clean her room, she noticed suddenly.

Cora shook her head, trying to get it to focus on the right things. Costume, makeup, driving. That's what she needed to focus on. Not cleaning her room, of all the chores.

She took a deep breath, and that helped.

"Right," she told herself. "Costume, makeup, driving. Let's go, Cora."

CORA FOUND herself very confused when she knocked on the door of the apartment she was supposed to be joining Elena. She wasn't sure whose apartment this was, but it was a nice complex.

There was absolutely no sound coming from inside, but there was some light coming through the blinds. She pulled her phone out from under the sheet that was the majority of her costume, double checking that she was at the right place, and knocked again.

After what felt like an eternity, the door swung open, revealing Elena's grinning face. Elena welcomed her into the apartment with a wide arm.

As she stepped over the threshold, the apartment burst into life. Classmates and friends popped up from behind every possible piece of furniture in the combined living room and kitchen.

"Surprise!" The group yelled. "Happy birthday!"

Their sudden appearance and screaming startled a small shriek from Cora, making her fumble the phone that was still in her hand. Elena laughed so hard she snorted, making the rest of the room burst into laughter as well.

Cora walked into the apartment and realized it was absolutely packed. Elena pressed a quick kiss to her cheek and attempted to move away. Cora grabbed her hand, not letting her escape that quickly.

"Oh, no, you don't! Come back here, you evil mastermind."

Elena laughed and acquiesced. She was dressed in a 1950's outfit - a pink pencil skirt with a black poodle embroidered on it and a black crop top. She'd even curled her long hair into pin curls.

"You beautiful mastermind," she added, fluttering

her eyelashes. "Did you plan all of this, Elena? It's wonderful!"

It really was. Cora was elated.

There were hopefully-fake spiderwebs all over the ceilings and lamps, pumpkins and jack-o-lanterns on every possible surface, and within a minute of entering the house, there was some sort of dance music with a great beat playing.

Elena didn't get a chance to answer. Cora set down her bag and found herself immediately enveloped in a crushing hug that smelled like too much musky yet woodsy cologne - Luís's favorite.

"Help!" she choked playfully. "Dying! Can't breathe!"

She felt his chest shake in a low chuckle. Her nose had gone directly into his armpit, one of the perks of their height difference of more than a foot.

"Seriously, Luís! Let me go, would you?"

The man opened his arms wide, allowing her to escape his embrace. She did so, then punched him lightly in the shoulder.

"Holy cologne, Batman! It's good to see you, but give a girl some warning."

"Sorry!" He rubbed his hand over his short cropped hair. "Welcome to Casa de Luís, birthday girl!"

"This is your place? It looks great!"

"Elena and Ebony did most of the decorating, but I did most of the food."

He waved a large hand at the kitchen which was overflowing with orange and black serving dishes.

"And it's not even poisoned," Elena bragged on her older brother.

Cora turned back to see her beaming with pride. She wagged a finger at her girlfriend playfully.

"You are sneaky, madame."

Elena poked her chest gently.

"And you almost ruined it by forgetting! You would have been literally ghosting your own party, instead of being a ghost hunter at it."

Cora felt herself blush in embarrassment and grimaced.

"I really am sorry about that, Elena. I wasn't trying to ghost the party. I honestly lost track of the time."

Elena waved off the apology with one hand, grabbing Cora's with the other.

"I know. You aren't the ghosting type. Now come and eat and say hello to everyone!"

～

SPOOKY SOUNDS and laughter filled the apartment, punctuated by the bass line of their music. After Cora's arrival, they had flung the door to Luis's apartment wide open and invited the neighbors to join them. It had turned into the apartment version of a block party, with music and furniture spilling out into the open-ended hallway.

"Happy birthday! A stranger called to her, tipping their cup in her direction.

"Thanks!" she called back.

The late night air was crisp, and Cora was glad that she hadn't worn the ghost costume. Unsurprisingly, Elena had managed to find somewhere to get away from the noise of the party. Cora wanted to check in on her and make sure that her anxiety wasn't bothering her too much.

The sound and press of bodies a little overwhelming, even for her.

Cora checked each of the rooms in Luis's apartment, searching for Elena. She was amused to find her roommate making out with a guy that Cora didn't recognize in Luis's spare room. She looked up when Cora entered the room and gave her a thumbs up before turning her attention back to her partner.

Assured she was having a good time, Cora left the room the same way she found it, continuing her search. Elena wasn't in the restroom or anywhere in the kitchen. It figured that she would've found her way outside, even on a night as cool as this one.

Peeking her head around the corner of the staircase, she spotted a familiar 50s silhouette watching over the apartment complex. Elena was always beautiful, but damn, Cora loved her in this outfit. With a grin, she leaned on the railing next to her girlfriend. She even had the perfect pick up line for the occasion.

"Hey, you got a quarter?"

"What?"

Cora asked the question again, looking up at Elena's perfect, confused face in the warm light of the single streetlight on this side of the building.

"Do you have a quarter?"

Elena's coral lips were pursed, her eyebrows drawn together in confusion when she responded.

"Uh, maybe in my purse? Why do you need a quarter?"

She looked past Cora, as if someone else was actually asking for a quarter. Cora hit her with her cheesiest grin when their eyes, and finished the pick up line.

"'Cause I want to call my mother and tell her I met the woman of my dreams."

Elena burst into laughter, scaring a few people that were coming up the stairs.

"You are absolutely ridiculous, you know that?"

Cora batted her eyelashes at her.

"Being ridiculous is one of my best qualities, as you well know. You doing okay out here?"

"Oh yeah, I just needed some space. There's a lot of people in the apartment, and it's a nice night."

"It's maybe 45 degrees out here," Cora pointed out. "Only you would define this as a nice night."

She shrugged her broad shoulders, turning her face back to the view of the Greensboro skyline. Cora could see her smile was still on her face.

"I'm really sorry I was late tonight, Elena. I'll be better about setting alarms for myself. This party turned out really great, despite me."

"Lucky for you that tonight, you were the guest of honor. Otherwise we would've partied without you," Elena teased. "But it's also not over yet! We haven't done cake or presents!"

"I didn't realize there was cake!"

"Cora! Who throws a birthday party without cake? I even made your favorite."

Cora gasped in delight.

"You made me hummingbird cake?"

"Sure did! I also made some lemon pound cake just in case people couldn't eat pecans, but the hummingbird cake is specifically for you."

Cora couldn't resist wrapping her arms around Elena's thick waist and squeezing her against her body.

"You are literally my favorite person in the entire world!" she squealed.

Elena hugged her back, and pressed a kiss to her cheek.

"And you're mine. Happy early birthday, Cora."

They made their way back into the crowded

apartment, still arm in arm. Elena only let Cora go to reach the cake from its safe safe on top of the refrigerator.

Cora inhaled the smell of the cream cheese frosting and the crumbled pecans on the top and smiled. This pineapple spice cake always made her feel like it was still the middle of summer, which was why she loved it for her birthday.

"Cake time, everybody! Get in here!" Luis boomed, making the people around him jump. It didn't take much to bring the rest of the college students into the apartment. Elena used his lighter to light the large, glittery number candles on the cake.

Once it seemed like everyone was more or less in the room, Elena's brother led them in singing the birthday song.

The group's rendition was horribly off key and lacked any real sort of harmony. Cora loved every second of it.

"And many moooooore," the group finished. The room whooped and cheered.

"Make a wish!" Elena whispered excitedly.

Cora closed her eyes and thought hard.

I wish for many more birthdays like this one, surrounded by my favorite people.

She had a feeling that this wish would be coming true, and she couldn't wait. She looked up at Elena, grabbed her face gently and pulled her into a deep kiss. The crowd hooted.

"Now, who wants some cake?" Cora asked, to more cheers.

THE END

Halloween Present

"HOLY SHIT, what the hell happened in here?"

Cora's stunned voice broke Elena out of her frenzy.

Elena blinked. The room around her was absolute chaos, with pieces of clothing strewn everywhere, falling from the floor to the bed and creating

Elena's chest was tight, and her stomach churned. She turned to look at Cora, whose face would have fit in well in a cartoon. Her eyes were wide and her jaw was slack with shock.

"Elena, are you okay? What is going on?"

She could feel herself starting to hyperventilate, and tried to blurt out why before she lost the ability to speak.

"I just found out we're having an office Halloween party, and I have absolutely nothing to wear and everyone is going to hate me and think I'm a stick in the mud--"

She knew in the back of her head that it was ridiculous to go into a full-blown anxiety attack over Halloween costume, but she couldn't do anything to stop it on her own. She could feel Cora assessing her and realizing what was happening.

"Whoa, okay, slow down. Come here."

Cora offered Elena her hands, and Elena placed her shaky ones in them. With a squeeze, Cora started rubbing circles into the backs of her hands.

"I'm here," she said in an even, soothing voice. "I've got you. Do you feel my hands on yours?"

Elena took a shaky breath and nodded.

"Okay, I want you to breathe in every time I start a circle. Can you do that?"

Elena nodded again, and her girlfriend started counting as she watched Elena carefully to make sure she breathed properly. Each circle lasted for a count of three, and helped to loosen the muscles in her chest enough to make the next breath easier.

Slowly but surely, Elena could feel herself calming down. When her breathing was more reasonable, she pulled her hands from Cora's. She sat on the floor amidst the clothing she'd flung everywhere. The smaller woman followed her to the floor, crossing her legs underneath her.

She was still watching Elena carefully, but her face was less etched with concern now that Elena was breathing.

"Do you want to talk about it?" She asked carefully.

Elena nodded, but took a few more deep breaths before answering.

"Right. I found out we're having a Halloween party at work next week."

Cora grimaced sympathetically.

"I'm so sorry they sprung that on you! That sucks, Elena."

"It gets worse. Costumes are mandatory, and they're book themed, and I have nothing to wear."

"Okay, so next question. Do you have to go?"

Elena shook her head. She could feel her lips quivering and hated it.

"Do you want to go? Do you think it would be fun?"

She thought about it, swallowing hard before she answered.

"I think I do," she whispered. "It'd be fun to hang out with my coworkers outside of work."

"I think that sounds fun, too," Cora said with a smile. "So do you have any ideas?"

Elena shook her head again, feeling her heart start to race again.

"That's okay. It's book themed. We can work with that. There are a lot of books to choose from."

She hated the swell of panic that came with that many choices.

"But I don't have anything to wear, and I don't know any book characters that I could dress as."

"I'm sure we can come up with something together. You have a great wardrobe, and I'm sure there's something in here that we can make work."

"You don't think it's a lost cause?"

Cora leaned forward to tuck a stray lock of hair behind Elena's ear for her, grazing her cheek with the backs of her fingers. Elena felt her face curl into a smile.

"Not at all. We're here together, and we have a week. We will make it work."

Elena leaned into Cora, allowing herself to relax for the first time since she'd come home.

"You're the best, you know that?"

Cora grinned, and brushed more tendrils of hair away from her girlfriend's face.

"I know. Now, what do you need to be calm and comfortable? Do you need a cup of tea or lemonade or something? The weighted blanket?"

Elena sat quietly for a moment, taking stock of what state her body was in.

"I think a cup of tea would be nice," she decided. "Do we have any of the peppermint left?"

Cora rose from the floor gracefully and offered a hand to the larger woman.

"Let's go and find out, shall we?"

Elena accepted, using the bed as an anchor for her other hand. She gestured to the chaotic wreck that their normally pristine bedroom had turned into.

"Shouldn't we clean this up first?"

"Nope. I'm gonna take care of you, and then we can deal with this."

TEN MINUTES LATER, Elena felt like she could breathe again for the first time in over an hour. She inhaled the steam from her mug of tea, enjoying the herbal and minty smell that surrounded her in their apartment's tiny kitchen. Cora had made herself a cup of hot cocoa, and was sitting quietly on the barstool next to her, contentedly swirling the mini marshmallows into the drink.

Elena watched her silently for a few minutes, taking sips of tea as she watched the small globs of sugar dissolve into the cocoa. She loved the way the hot drink made her mouth feel cooler and cleaner. It was exactly what she needed after the panic attack.

"Sorry I freaked out on you."

Cora tilted her head up to meet Elena's eyes. The

cool LED lights in the kitchen made her fair skin and blonde curls look almost luminescent, and brought out hints of green in her brown eyes.

"It's all right," she said simply. "You've had a lot going on the last few weeks, and I know how much unexpected parties stress you out."

"Yeah, but still. What a useless thing to have a panic attack over, right?"

Cora laughed.

"I'm fairly certain that no one has ever gone into a panic attack over something that actually works panicking over," she pointed out. "It's usually just the last straw that sends you over the edge."

"Yeah, but still. A Halloween costume?"

"Babe, you know brains don't make sense. It's really all right. I'm just glad I was able here to help you through it. Not that I'm glad that it happened, but… You know what I mean."

And she did. It was always easier coming down from a panic attack with somebody else around, especially when that someone else knew exactly how to help you."

"I'm glad you were here to help me through it, too, Cora."

"What else are girlfriends for?"

Cora asked the question rhetorically, then smirked.

"What?" Elena asked, curious.

"Well, I can think of one other thing girlfriends are for."

"Oh?"

Cora leaned forward and planted a kiss on Elena's lips that tasted of chocolate and sugar. Elena couldn't resist the giggle that bubbled through her lips.

"You are absolutely ridiculous, you know that?"

Cora raised a thin blonde eyebrow at the question and beamed, affecting a posh, old-fashioned accent.

"But of course, darling! It's one of my finest qualities."

They both dissolved into peals of laughter, leaning into each other on their wooden bar stools. They went back to their drinks and the quiet of the kitchen. Everything was starting to feel like it was actually going to be okay, just the way that Elena wanted it to be.

After they finished their drinks, Cora and Elena Made their way to the doorway of their bedroom, staring at the mess in front of them.

"So, I've got to ask…. Was there something in particular you were looking for when you did all of this?"

Elena crossed her arms in front of her chest, surveying the damage.

"Would you believe me if I said I have absolutely no idea?"

"Looking at this room… yes. I would. Let's start with the tried and true tenet of my room cleaning policy - make a path to the closet."

"The fact that you even have a room cleaning policy explains so much about you."

Cora grinned up at her.

"C'mon. Let's get to work. We can get this room back into shape without much of a fuss, I think."

Without further ado, the petite, slim woman Rolled up the sleeves of her flannel over shirt and got to work picking up the clothes that had been flung everywhere.

CORA HAD BEEN RIGHT. The two of them had made short work of the mess she'd made, even pulling out a few items that she had forgotten she owned and put them in an empty Amazon box to donate or resell later.

The room was even cleaner than it had been before she got home from work, turning it back into a space that made her feel at ease and peaceful. The woman next to her had a lot to do with that, and Elena was struck with a sincere sense of gratefulness for her.

"Cora?" she called softly.

She turned her head towards Elena, a curl flopping into her eyes.

"Hm?"

"You are literally my favorite person in the world, you know that?"

The corners of her mouth quirked up into a smile that emphasized her apple-like cheeks that were now bright pink.

"And you're mine, Elena."

They both sat on the bed, smiling at each other for several heartbeats.

"So, you need a bookish Halloween costume," Cora said matter-of-factly, breaking the silence. Did your coworkers give you any hints on what they were going to do?"

"Apparently the boss and his wife always dress up as The Old Man and The Sea, and it's a sight to behold, but that's all I've got to work with."

"How... No, I'll just have to see it. Okay, so typically kids books offer the best options for costumes..."

She thought for a moment.

"How about Amelia Bedelia?"

"You don't think it's a little stereotypical for a Latina to dress up as a maid? All my white bread coworkers don't need that image of me in their heads."

"Ugh, that's true. Hester Prynne?"

Before Elena could respond, Cora waved that suggestion away.

"No, that's also stereotypical in a gross way. How about some characters from Matilda?"

"Nah, Madame Trunchbull is yet another fatphobic character. Dahl was super bigoted. I'm not doing that."

"Damn. That is a fair point. Hmmm….."

Cora tapped her chin thoughtfully.

"I mean, there's always Harry Potter."

"Yeah, but I don't have any of the stuff for Harry Potter costume. I mean, I maybe have the shoes. They just wear regular shoes, right?"

Cora fell back on the bed laughing.

"Yes, they just wear regular shoes in Harry Potter, you weirdo."

"But also JK Rowling continues to be the worst in pretty much every possible way, so I don't want to dress up as her characters either."

"Ugh. Why is choosing a costume so hard?"

"Because I'm fat and brown-skinned," Elena said matter-of-factly. "And because I care about what I want to wear. If I looked like you, I would have much less of a problem. I could just go and grab something off the shelf. But I'm not, so."

She shrugged.

"It sucks."

"Yup. But it's the way it is, so for now we have to work with it. I'm gonna have another cup of tea. Do you want any?"

"Nah. I'm gonna sit here and do some research on what we can do."

Cora whipped her phone out and typed furiously. Elena pulled herself up from the bed and gathered her cardigan around herself. It was chilly in the apartment.

She detoured to the thermostat on her way to the kitchen, turning the heat on. It was in the mid-60s. If Elena was cold, Cora had to be freezing. She refilled the electric kettle and waited for the whistle of hot water.

She rinsed out her favorite bright orange mug from the earlier drink, and put in a new bag of tea. When the kettle whistled, she began to pour.

Elena nearly spilled the boiling water down the front of herself when Cora came running into the kitchen, squealing. Her face was alight and her hands flapping as she flew in.

"I've got it! I've got the perfect costume for you!"

"What is it? What's the costume?"

"Okay, well, first I gotta tell you how I got inspired. Come back to the bedroom."

"Gimme a second to set a timer. My tea needs to steep before I can drink it."

"Okay, well hurry up!"

She dashed back down the hallway, still squealing with happiness. Elena laughed and set a timer on her phone before sliding it back into her cardigan pocket.

She made her way back into their bedroom to discover that clothes once again covered their queen sized bed.

"Cora, we just cleaned this!" she groaned.

"No, I know! But look at what's on the bed, Elena."

She narrowed her focus to the individual pieces on the bed, trying to make it look a little bit less like a mess.

She saw a pair of red pumps sitting on top of a black maxi skirt that she knew had a slit up the middle. Next to it, sat a white wool sweater with a pink heart knitted into it, and a full-length crimson coat that she was pretty sure one of her tears had bought at a thrift store several years before.

"Okay, this is a cute outfit, but I'm not seeing a Halloween costume here."

Cora's hands were clasped together in glee.

"I'll give you one hint, okay? Alice in Wonderland."

It was like a lightbulb went off in Elena's head. She gasped.

"Of course! It's the queen of hearts! Cora, you're a genius!"

The sight of Cora bouncing with joy made Elena's heart clench in her chest in a good way.

"Isn't it great? There's like two or three things that you need to make it all come together, but with a little bit of makeup and a crown? It will be just perfect!"

"It's already perfect," Elena told her. "I can't believe you just came up with this out of my closet."

"You've got a great closet, babe. If I tried this in my own closet it would not have worked."

"You also don't have any coworkers to spring parties on or have parties sprung upon you by."

Cora shrugged.

"Also true, but that's besides the point. This is all yours, Elena, just like me."

"Come here and let me kiss you."

Cora obliged with a grin.

OVER THE NEXT FEW DAYS, Elena kept catching Cora returning from thrift and craft stores with small things to add to the costume - some fake roses, a tiny Gold crown, and miscellaneous small hearts to really make the costume pop. The only thing that she had not seen was Cora's costume. She had asked several times, but always been told that she would have to wait and see.

By the time the night of the party arrived, Elena was fairly certain that she would have the best costume out of all of her new coworkers. She still had no idea what they were going to dress up as, but she didn't care. Tonight was all about getting to know her coworkers outside the bounds of their office requirements, and introducing them to Cora. It was going to be wonderful. she could already tell.

Elena knocked on the bedroom door, which she had been banished from while her girlfriend got ready for the party.

"just a second!" Cora called. Elena sighed impatiently.

"Are you almost ready for your debut? Two of us have to get ready for this party, you know."

She kept her voice light and teasing as she leaned on the door, trying to be patient.

"Yeah, yeah, I hear you."

The door jerked open a moment later, causing Elena to stumble into the room. Cora gasped and tried, unsuccessfully, to catch her. They both tumbled to the floor in a heap.

"Sorry! I didn't realize you were leaning on the door!"

Elena grumbled under her breath as she pulled herself into a sitting position. She caught a glimpse of her girlfriend and had to do a double take.

"Whoa. You look amazing."

She wore a tea length dusty Carolina blue gown that looked like it was actually made of silk, complete with a delicate lacy apron that tied behind her. She had pulled her chin-length blonde curls away from her face with a simple black bow headband, and tied the look together with a pair of white stocking tights. She was a perfectly elegant Alice in Wonderland.

"Always the tone of surprise!" Cora quipped, but her cheeks colored a sweet pink.

"Seriously, babe, your costume is *amazing*."

"Why thank you! I have had years of Halloween parties moving me towards this day. One might even call me the Halloween Queen!"

"You are not the Halloween Queen. But you are an awesome Alice in Wonderland."

"And I even fell over! At least it wasn't down a rabbit hole," Cora laughed.

Elena glanced at her watch and grinned wickedly, unable to resist another reference.

"If we don't hurry, we are going to be very late for a very important date."

Cora looked at her phone and squeaked.

"Ah, you're right! I'm gonna go do my makeup while you get dressed, then I'm ready to go when you are!"

"I still have to do the whole face thing!" Elena called after her as she darted into the bathroom.

They had come up with a way to pull the heart-shaped theme into her makeup - Elena was going to use some of Cora's powder foundation to create a pale heart that stretched around her eyebrows and came to a point at her chin. If it hadn't been for a costume, Elena knew she would never have done something this extravagant of her own volition.

They had tested it, though, and it made the entire costume come together. They both knew she would need help with it to get it to look perfect.

Strangely, Elena found that she wasn't nervous about the party anymore as she got dressed. She was just excited, the way that she figured a neurotypical person would have been from the start. She could at least be grateful that she had gotten there before she actually got to the party. It didn't always happen that way.

Cora had added a marigold and black tulle tutu under the slitted maxi skirt to give it volume. The poof and color added a little more dimension to the costume. Elena found the scratch of tulle against her skin to be one of the most irritating sensations known to man, so she had added a pair of black leggings to the underside of the ensemble.

The thick wool sweater kept her upper body comfortably warm, and the long red coat tied everything together, literally and figuratively. She left the coat unbuttoned, but tied the belt around her waist to emphasize her waist. All that was left was her makeup and her shoes, and she would be ready to go to her first ever party at work.

ELENA COULD HEAR the rumble of the bass from the packed parking lot of the party destination restaurant. She hadn't realized this was gonna be quite so hopping.

"You ready?" Cora asked from the driver's seat.

"Ready as I'll ever be!"

"Just remember, you say the word and we'll go. I'll fake a stomach ache or an emergency and we'll be out of there in less than five minutes. I've got your back."

Elena smiled gratefully at the love of her life.

"Thanks, Cora. Same goes for you, if you get overwhelmed."

She beamed.

"Now, let's go party!"

The noise was more than a little overwhelming once

they got into the restaurant. Cora squeezed Elena's hand, and she smiled back. Standing tables had been placed around the room with long, trailing tablecloths with cobweb doilies at the center. A black ceramic cauldron sat on each table with fog billowing out throughout the room. Waiters wearing witch and wizard costumes wove through the room carrying trays of spooky looking hors d'oeuvres.

Elena had to laugh out loud when she caught sight of her boss.

True to the rumor, he and his wife had dressed up as the old man and the sea. The middle-aged, balding man wore a bright purple Hawaiian shirt tucked into a pair of khaki shorts, kept firmly in place with a pair of bright red suspenders that matched the rain boots that covered his feet. In his hand, he held a gnarled old cane fishing pole that had clearly seen better days. Next to him, a plump, statuesque woman she presumed was his wife wore a tight turquoise gown with plush sea creatures attached all over it. She pulled the full look together with a headband that looked like the crest of a wave. She had to admit it was pretty impressive, especially for a book that really didn't inspire a costume.

"Elena! You made it!" the old man crowed, startling Cora. "Happy Halloween!"

"Happy halloween, Mr. Sturgess! I love your costume!"

"I have already told you time and again to call me Ron, Elena," he scolded her with a mock glare. She felt Cora failing to suppress a giggle beside her. He turned "And who is this lovely lady?"

"Yes, sir. Cora, this is my boss, Ron Sturgess, Esquire. Ron, this my girlfriend Cora."

"Ah, the girlfriend!" he tapped a finger to his temple and winked at them. "I should've guessed."

"It's a pleasure to meet you, sir."

Cora dropped into a curtsy that made the older man cackle, and made Elena's jaw drop.

"When did you learn how to curtsy?"

"My mom sent me to etiquette lessons. Don't worry about it."

Cora turned her attention back to the law partner.

"Now, Ron, you haven't introduced us to your companion. I assume this must be Mrs. Sturgess?"

"Call me Stacey, dears. Everyone else does. Welcome to the party!"

All of Stacey's words stuck together as if they were connected by a trail of warm honey.

"It's a pleasure to meet you, Stacey! I've heard so many wonderful things about you."

The older woman threw her head back and laughed.

"You'll hear the real stuff once you've been here longer. Now, what can I get y'all to drink?"

"Why don't you show me what you've got, Stacey? I'm a bit picky with what I drink."

"Come right this way, sugar. I'm sure there's something drinkable in here for you. We'll be back in just a second, Ron!"

She steered Cora towards the back of the room where the drinks must be. Ron peeked around her and his eyes lit up.

"Actually, I see someone else I must go chat with, Elena. I will catch back up with you in a jiffy. Have some food! Find those coworkers of yours"

As if on cue, the two scrawny white men that Elena spent all day with sidled up on either side of her, both looking remarkably similar to what they had worn during the workday.

"You look *amazing!* You're definitely the Queen of the Office!" Adam exclaimed

"That costume is like a work of art, but I'm pretty sure all of that is actually your clothes? How did you do that?" Quincy scratched his head under his bowler in confusion.

"Thanks! My girlfriend put it together for me," she announced proudly. "As for you two... did y'all even bother with costumes? Let me guess, Quincy is Atticus Finch and ... I can't even tell what you are, Adam. You just look like you."

Both men clutched their chests as if she'd mortally wounded them with her words.

"I'm not Atticus Finch," Quincy protested loudly. "Look at the sunglasses and the cigarette! I'm clearly Hunter S. Thompson!"

He pulled up a picture on his phone, and she could see the resemblance. He wore a black and white striped polo, khaki shorts and a black bowler hat. He had a pair of Dahmer glasses resting on the tip of his nose, and a cigarette that had never been lit hanging out of the side of his mouth.

"Okay, I see it now. I'm game. And what about you, Adam?"

"I am clearly the Great Gatsby, Elena. Come on now! Look at me"

She squinted at him skeptically.

"You're wearing the same suit you wore to work today, Adam. You just slicked back your hair and called it a costume. We'll call it a valiant attempt."

Quincy guffawed and slapped his friend hard on the back.

"I told you, man! It's all in the accessories."

"Well we can't all be drop dead gorgeous Queens like her royal highness over there, now can we?"

"Why, I think we could make you look great in a dress, Adam! I've got just the thing for your peach skin tone," Stacey drawled.

The men whirled to find Stacey and Cora grinning at them, each holding two drinks.

"You must be Cora!" Quincy yelped. "It's so good to meet you! Elena's told us all about you."

"Yeah, and most of it's even been good!" Adam added, then yelped when Quincy elbowed him in the ribs to shut him up. Cora and Elena both laughed. Cora moved closer

"It's nice to meet you two as well! I have also heard mostly good things," Cora said with a wink. "Babe, I brought you a rum and coke."

She took the drink, brushing her fingers against Cora's. Elena laughed when she realized that the ice cubes were shaped like skulls.

"A good choice! Thanks, hon."

She pressed a kiss to Cora's cheek and they turned towards the men together. She felt a little less anxious with the weight of a drink in her hand, and with her coworkers around them.

"Dude, you guys have the best costumes *ever*," Adam whined. "How come girls get the best costumes?"

"Cause they make an effort. Rum and coke sounds delicious. I'm gonna go get one," Quincy declared. "You want one?"

"Oh, sure."

Quincy made his way to the bar and back within minutes with drinks in hand. When he had everyone's attention, he raised his glass.

"Let's toast to a spooky rest of the year with new friends!"

"To new friends!" they all echoed, clinking their cups together.

THE END

Halloween Future

IT WAS Halloween night and Cora and Elena's home had devolved into complete and utter chaos, thanks to the three children that were in the process of getting ready for the evening's festivities. Elena stood in the doorway watching with baby Theo in her arms, bouncing lightly on the balls of her feet to help him stay asleep.

The six-month-old was the only one who was already ready for the trick or treating. Dressed in a Tootsie Roll costume, he would be staying with Cora and help him to hand out candy to any trick-or-treaters that came by, while Marianne and Elena wrangled the older kids.

"Why can't tía Cora come trick or treating with us?" David whined from under his fireman's hat. His mother was crouched in front of him, trying to apply face paint to help make him look like his favorite Paw Patrol character.

"Stop squirming, David. You're gonna mess up your whiskers!" Marianne wiped her forehead on the back of her arm and dipped the paintbrush into the paint pot again.

He held still for a few seconds before trying to turn his head again to look at where Cora was helping his sister Sofía into her fall colored fairy costume.

"Cora isn't coming with us because she can't walk very far right now without getting tired."

"Is it because of the baby?"

"Yes, tía Cora doesn't walk very well because she's going to have a baby very soon, just like I did with Theo. Remember?"

"Ohhhh…"

He scrunched up his face and his mother fixed him with a glare that made his eyes go wide.

"Pick a face to make and keep it there for another minute so that I can finish making you look like Marshall, please!"

"Sorry, Mama."

He sighed as if his life were the most difficult thing in the world. She suppose that it probably was pretty difficult for a five-year-old hold still while his mother put makeup on his face, but he had asked for this, so she had very little sympathy for the small boy.

Sofía on the other hand could not wait for her makeup. Cora had started painting glittery leaves all over the girl's face to tie into the very costume that she had begged for. Elena knew that her nine-year-old niece would love the final effect, but she was pretty sure that she would find flecks of glitter paint everywhere for months to come. She wasn't entirely looking forward to that part of it, but there was very little that she wouldn't do for her niblings.

It would also be good practice, since Cora was due to give birth to twins in less than two weeks. Elena's sister-in-law had been coming to visit once or twice a week for the last month, helping to make sure that the house was as baby ready as it could be and to impart her motherly wisdom upon the two wives. When she learned that her own neighborhood would not be allowing kids to go trick or treating in it, she had declared it a sign that she was supposed to bring the kids with her to visit their favorite tías.

Elena knew that Cora was grateful for the help, and for the company. She had been put on bed rest at 36 weeks pregnant, and while it hadn't stopped her from working, it had made her more than a little bit antsy. With Elena working more hours than ever to prepare for her own maternity leave once the baby came, Marianne's warm company had been a blessing for them both.

Theo woke with a happy burble, reaching his arms up for Elena's shoulder-length black curls. She smiled down at the child in her arms, and placed her index finger in his chubby palm instead.

"How's that, buddy? Isn't that better than pulling tía's hair out?"

He blew a spit bubble at her, and she laughed.

"All right, David! You're all set. Go play until we're ready to go."

He didn't have to be told twice. He scampered out of the office-turned-nursery and back into the living room where all of his toy cars and track were. It looked like Cora was almost done with Sofía's face paint as well. She looked like a beautiful Puerto Rican wood nymph as she stood with one hand on her slim hip in front of Cora. Her mother crouched behind her, adjusting the way that the wings she wore sat against her back.

With one final flourish, Cora leaned back against the crib she'd been using his back support while she worked.

"You are officially magical, Sofía," she declared. "Go look in the mirror and tell me what you think."

The girl flew off down the hallway and all three women heard a delighted gasp and then a high-pitched squeal.

"I'm *beautiful*," she yelled back to them. They traded amused glances and smiles.

Cora twisted her back, and Elena heard cracks and pops that made Marianne grimace. Theo let go of Elena's finger, and made grabbing motions at his mother, who took him and started making silly faces at him. Elena handed him over to Marianne with a sigh, then turned her attention to her wife, who was gathering up her painting supplies.

"Do you need some help getting up, love?"

Cora looked at the light hardwood floor, wrinkling her button nose in distaste at its shiny surface.

"Yes, please," she grumbled. "I cannot wait until I can actually function as a human being again on my own."

Marianne and Elena laughed. Elena walked over to where her wife sat cross-legged on the floor, and offered her hands to her with a gentle smile.

"You did the hard work with the painting. Let me deal with the mess. Let's get you into a more comfortable chair, shall we?"

Cora smiled up at her tiredly, and took Elena's hands. She hoisted herself up into a crouch, balancing herself with Elena's hands, and then rose to her full height.

Elena looked over her very pregnant wife, but her eyes caught on the print on her black maternity t-shirt.

"Cora, is that your halloween costume?"

The pregnant woman grinned, showing off all of her teeth.

"Yes, yes it is. Do you like it?"

"Why? What is it?" Marianne asked.

Elena laughed when Marianne looked at the shirt for the first time and her jaw dropped. Where her round stomach extended from the rest of her body, the design of a magic 8 ball had been printed. It was such a Cora costume.

"That is brilliant!" Marianne cackled. "I wish I'd thought of that!"

"Now, when people ask me when I'm due, I can shake my belly and give them a nonsensical answer from the magic 8 ball, and they'll just have to accept it. It's much better than having to listen to their ridiculous advice about pregnancy like I've been doing for the last 38 weeks. I'll just shake my belly a little and answer them."

"Just be careful not to shake them so hard they decide it's time to be born, okay?" Elena cautioned. "I don't want to have to come running home because you shook yourself into labor."

Cora flapped a hand at Elena.

"I won't. And even if I do, the baby bag is all packed and in the car, so we're as prepared as we can be."

"Yes, but I don't want to be there in the delivery room in a witch costume."

"But think of how funny the story would be for later, Elena! We would have the best giving birth story ever!"

Elena started rubbing her forehead while she shook her head, laughing.

"You are the most ridiculous woman that I have ever met."

"And you love me!" Cora chirped, still beaming up at her wife.

A shutter sound surprised them both, and they turned to look at Marianne with questioning looks on their faces. She shrugged, unconcerned with their attention.

"You guys are too cute to not take pictures of. Plus, Anton wanted an update."

"Tell him he sucks for having to work tonight."

"Oh believe me, I have. The kids were also very vocal about it before we left. Speaking of the kids, I'm gonna go make sure they eat some real food before they have access to unlimited candy."

"Oh, dinner sounds good," Cora murmured. "Do we have anything made?"

"No, I'm ordering from the Mexican place down the street. I didn't want to leave you guys with a bunch of dishes. Would you like me to order you something?"

"Oh, I love El Cazador's choripollo! Make that my order, please!" Cora chirped excitedly.

Elena smirked.

"You know they have other food there, right?"

"Yes, but it's *delicious*. Why would I order something that I don't know if I'll like when the choripollo is just that good?"

"Fair enough. I'll have the arroz texano."

Marianne smiled at their argument, her phone in her hand.

"I'll go order for everyone then!"

Elena walked with Cora to the living room, where the kids were playing. A small white terrier watched them curiously from the couch, her tail wagging slowly.

Cora sank onto the couch with a groan. The terrier hopped onto her lap, curling up against her round belly.

She ran her fingers through her fur, gently scratching her scalp. Elena watched her family with what she was sure was a goofy smile on her face, wondering how she had gotten so lucky to call all of them her family.

THE END

The Wedding

This short story has never been seen before, but features the wedding ceremony for Cora and Elena. I hope you love reading it as much as I loved writing it.

The Wedding

CORA FELT like royalty as she stood in front of the altar, waiting for her bride to make her first appearance. The blush silk jumpsuit she wore felt like water against her skin, and the white lace veil that draped from just below her eyes to her shoulders to create a capelet was the perfect wedding-y addition.

She had thought she would be nervous, standing in front of so many people with nothing to fidget with while the music played, but all she could think about was how happy she was that everyone had made it for this moment.

Deciding to hold their wedding on December 27th had been a bold choice, one that had worried them all as the RSVP dates crept closer together. They had expected that people would have Christmas travel plans and that some people would miss their big day, which is why they had planned to hold a second reception at their home after the New Year.

Both Cora and Elena had nearly wept with joy when every single one of their invited guests had been able to attend. Across the table, their mothers had nearly wept with anxiety as they stared at their planning spreadsheets and tried to make sure they had ordered enough of everything.

Cora had been glad for it then, and she was still glad of it now. This refurbished barn in the middle of Virginia was packed to the rafters with people that loved them. What could be better than that?

But she was even gladder when Sofia stepped into view with her frilly gold ballgown, white faux fur stole and her golden basket of ivy leaves. She took her duties as flower girl and ring bearer more seriously than Cora had ever seen her take anything, tossing small handfuls of the leaves with each slow step.

Her attention was drawn away when Ebony followed suit in the floor-length garnet velvet gown with a sweetheart neckline that highlighted her pear-shaped torso and broad shoulders. She strode confidently behind the flower girl with a quiet smile on her lips. A few steps behind her, my soon-to-be sister-in-law Marianne wore an almost identical gown. Instead of garnet, hers was emerald. It draped over her curvaceous chest and belly so differently from Ebony's, but as they lined up on either side of the aisle, it looked nearly perfect.

But when the aisle cleared, I had no time to look at either of them. The whole rest of the room went silent as the most beautiful woman I'd ever seen was walking down the aisle towards me.

Everything in the refurbished barn between us faded away, like a photo that had the background blurred out. Elena stood out, sharp and soft and stunning in a dress that Cora hadn't seen. The plunging neckline of the white ball gown might have been indecent, if not for the blush illusion-style lace that had covered her bodice and arms before trailing off in a rough hem around the top of her billowing skirt. It was a marvel, but it was just dressing on the true masterpiece.

Elena's brilliant smile, and a light application of makeup, turned her cheeks into rosy apples and her eyes to stars. She glided down the aisle with the grace of a ballerina. She directed all of that starlight at Cora, who was fairly certain that no one in the world had ever been as happy as she was in that moment.

***

THE CEREMONY HAD BEEN an enormous source of stress between Cora and Elena as they had worked to tie the Catholic elements that were important to Elena and her family in with the less religious parts that were important to Cora as the non-religious partner.

The only part that had been non-negotiable, that truly mattered to both of them was the writing of their own vows. They'd written what they wanted to say together, and then she had used her years of writing experience to make them short and snappy, without making them feel canned.

Honestly, though, they should have known that it wouldn't have really mattered which hymns were sung, or what order things went in. Cora couldn't have cared less about those details in the moment. All she cared about was the moment where she became a wife. Elena's wife.

Cora tripped through her own vows, stopping a few times to catch her breath, but she managed to get them out without full on sobbing with joy. All that stood between them now were Elena's. She had insisted on making some changes to the final version of her vows, so that Cora hadn't done all the work, and when she spoke, her voice was warm and sure. Her words rang out in the barn.

"So many things have changed in the last four years, but one thing has remained constant - you. Every day that I've spent with you has been better than the last, and I can't wait to see what tomorrow brings. I will revel in your successes with you, and I will lift you up when you are down. I promise I will be right next to you every step of the way, so long as we both shall live."

The vows were so similar to the ones she'd made, but so entirely right for Elena, too. Cora was sure that no one in the room was unaffected by the love in her voice. Even the pastor was a little choked up as they asked the most important question of the entire ceremony.

"Elena Maria Mendez, do you take this woman to be your lawfully wedded wife for a lifetime of tomorrows?"

"I do." Her eyes shone even more now, reflecting the twinkle of the lights wrapped around the beams and so much love that Cora's knees wobbled beneath her. When the pastor asked her the same question, she replied with breathless affirmation.

They beamed at the both of them before the final pronouncement of the ceremony. "I now pronounce you wife and wife. You may now kiss your bride."

Without a second's hesitation, Elena pulled Cora to her. The movement nearly lifted Cora off the ground, but she just wrapped her arms around Elena's neck and kissed her with reckless abandon.

When her feet touched the ground again, Cora couldn't help but feel as if the world had shifted just a little. The air around them felt brighter and warmer, even though she knew nothing had really changed.

They turned to face their audience with matching grins and gave a short bow before their exit music began to play. Cora and Elena were finally married and everything was right in their world. That deserved the celebration of a lifetime, and that is exactly what the evening had in store for them.

***

Afterword

So much has happened since I hit publish on Learning Curves. It was my first ever fiction publication and the first time I had really put my queer identity out into the world.

Writing these characters, Cora especially, helped me to figure out who I was. It helped me to come out to my friends and family, and even though some of that didn't go the way I wanted, I am so grateful for being able to do so. It helped me to make friends that have literally and figuratively changed my life in the best possible ways. It gave me the courage to leave my career as a journalist and try something new.

Since then, I have written more than a dozen separate stories - some under this name and some as Candace Harper. All of them have contained a little piece of me because I wrote Learning Curves.

I love these stories, every one of them. But I also know that these stories are not perfect. They need a thorough edit to be the best stories they can be, to give Cora and Elena the happily ever after they truly deserve.

But I love them for what they are, and if you're reading this, I hope you do, too.

I intend to rewrite this series into two novels in the future. It is already in the works, and I hope you'll be willing to read them when they're ready sometime next year.

For now, though, I'm just glad you're here at all. Thank you for being a part of this series.

About the Author

Ceillie Simkiss is a queer and neurodivergent author with her found family and furballs in the PNW.

She loves nothing more than curling up in bed with a book and her many furry creatures, but playing silly video games is a close second, even though she's terrible at them.

She also writes as Candace Harper. You can find all of her work on her website.

 twitter.com/foxglovefiction

 instagram.com/foxglovefiction

 bookbub.com/authors/ceillie-simkiss

www.ingramcontent.com/pod-product-compliance
Lightning Source LLC
Chambersburg PA
CBHW061209210726
48294CB00006B/1801